Five Nights at Freddy's

FAZBEAR FRIGHTS #2

FETCH

Five Nights at Freddy's™

FAZBEAR FRIGHTS #2

FETCH

SCOTT CAWTHON
ANDREA WAGGENER
CARLY ANNE WEST

Scholastic Inc.

Photo of TV static: © Klikk/Dreamstime

The publisher does not have any control over and does not assume any responsibility for author or third-party websites or their content.

This book is a work of fiction. Names, characters, places, and incidents are either the product of the author's imagination or are used fictitiously, and any resemblance to actual persons, living or dead, business establishments, events, or locales is entirely coincidental.

ISBN 978-1-338-57602-3

15 14   22 23 24

Printed in the U.S.A.

23

First printing 2020 • Book design by Betsy Peterschmidt

TABLE OF CONTENTS

FETCH

T he surf, the wind, and the rain were at war, battering against the old building so forcefully Greg wondered if its crumbling walls could stand against them. When the bawling thunder blasted the boarded-up window again Greg jumped back, stumbling into Cyril and tromping on his foot.

"Ow!" Cyril shoved Greg, jabbing his flashlight spastically at the wall in front of them. The light scanned over drooping sections of blue striped wallpaper and what looked like two red letters, "Fr." Streaks of something dark sprayed over the stripes. Was that pizza sauce? Or something else?

Hadi laughed at his two bumbling friends. "It's just the wind, guys. Suck it up."

Another gust hit the building, and the walls shuddered, drowning out Hadi's voice. The rain pounding on the metal roof ratcheted up, but inside the building, close by, something metallic clinked loud enough to be heard over the wind and rain.

"What was that?" Cyril whirled and swung his flashlight in a wild arc. At barely thirteen, Cyril was a year younger than Greg and Hadi, though still in their fledgling freshman class. He was short and skinny with boyish features and limp brown hair, and he had the misfortune of sounding like a cartoon mouse. It didn't win him many friends.

"'Let's go check out the old pizzeria,'" Cyril mimicked Greg's suggestion. "Yeah, this was a great idea."

It was a crisp autumn night, and the seaside town was dark, robbed of power by the latest storm's assault. Greg and his friends had planned a Saturday night of gaming and junk food, but as soon as the power went out, Hadi's parents tried to recruit them for a board game—the family's tradition during power outages. Hadi had convinced his parents to let the boys bike the short distance to Greg's house, where they could play one of Greg's new tabletop strategy games instead. But once there, Greg enlisted them to go to the pizzeria. For days he'd known he had to do this. It was like he was drawn to this place.

Or maybe he had it all wrong. This could be a wild goose chase.

Greg shined his flashlight around the corridor. They'd just explored the kitchen of the abandoned restaurant and had been shocked to find it was still stocked with pots, pans, and dishes. Who closed a pizzeria and left all that stuff behind?

After they left the kitchen, they found themselves next to a large stage at one end of what had once been the main eating area of the derelict pizzeria. A heavy black curtain at the back of the stage was drawn closed. None of the boys had volunteered to see what was behind the curtain . . . and none of them had mentioned seeing the curtain move when they passed the stage.

Hadi laughed again. "Better than hanging with the fam . . . hey, what's that?"

"What's what?" Cyril aimed his light in the direction of Hadi's gaze.

Greg turned his flashlight that way, too, toward the far corner of the large, table-filled room they stood in. The glowing beam landed on a row of hulking shapes lined up along a murky glass counter. Bright eyes reflected the light back at them from across the room.

"Cool," Hadi said, kicking aside a broken table leg as he made his way toward the counter.

Maybe, Greg thought, frowning at the eyes. One pair seemed to be staring right at him. Despite the confidence he'd felt before, he was beginning to wonder what exactly he was doing here.

Hadi approached the counter first. "This is dope!" He reached for something and sneezed when dust billowed up from the stand.

Before they left his house Greg had suggested they all take handkerchiefs to cover their noses and mouths, but he couldn't find any. He expected to find the empty restaurant filled with dust, mold, mildew, and who knew what else. Surprisingly, given the wet coastal climate, the only decay they'd seen was dust; but there was a lot of dust.

Greg stepped around an overturned metal chair and passed Cyril, who had his back pressed to a dirty, paint-peeled pillar in the middle of the dining area. Other than one broken table and two upside-down chairs, the area looked like it just needed a heavy cleaning before it could be fit for diners. Which, again, was strange. Greg had known *something* would be here, but he didn't expect the building to still hold dishes and furniture and . . . what else?

Greg looked at what Hadi held, and he sucked in his breath. Was this what he'd come for? Was this why the old place was calling to him?

"What is it?" Cyril asked, not moving any closer to the counter.

"I think it's a cat." Hadi turned the lumpy, roughly furred object he held. "Or maybe a ferret?" He poked at whatever it was. "Might be an animatronic?" He put it down and shined his light over the other shapes along the counter. "Yeah, awesome. They're prizes. See?" Hadi scanned his light over the stiff figures.

That explained the cavelike cubbyholes that lined the broad hallway Greg and his friends had come through to get to the dining area. The little enclosures must have been for arcade cabinets and game booths.

"I can't believe these are still here," Hadi said.

"Yeah." Greg frowned, studying what looked like a stiffened sea otter and a tangled octopus. Why were they still here?

The old pizzeria had stood, boarded up and bombarded by coastal storms and sea air, for who knew how long. The structure was clearly abandoned, and it looked not just old but ancient, on the verge of collapse. The graying, weathered siding was so faded you could barely tell what it was; the name of the pizzeria was long gone. So why did it look so good on the inside? Well, not *good*, exactly. But from where Greg stood, the building looked sturdy enough to stand another hundred years.

Greg and his parents had moved to the small town when he was in first grade, so he knew the place well. But he didn't really understand it. For example, he'd always thought it was strange that a boarded-up pizzeria had been left untouched in what was supposed to be a vacation spot. But then again, this wasn't exactly a swanky resort town. Greg's mom called it a "hodge podge." Big, fancy homes could be found across the street from tiny, ugly beach cabins draped in dirty fishing floats and surrounded by piles of old lumber or crumpled lawn furniture. The house across from Greg's had a huge boxy sedan, like from the seventies, up on blocks in the front yard. Still, Greg wondered why a pizza place couldn't be turned into something useful instead of being left a gnarled old ghost-building that practically screamed, "break in," to local kids.

But weirdly, it didn't look like anyone had broken in before Greg and Cyril and Hadi did. Greg had figured they'd find footprints, trash, graffiti—evidence that other "explorers" had been here before them. But . . . nothing. It was like the place was abandoned, dipped in formaldehyde, and preserved until Greg suddenly felt like he was supposed to come here.

"I bet these are still here because they're the really good prizes," Hadi said.

"No one ever wins the good prizes," Cyril piped up. He had edged a little closer to the counter, but he was still several feet away.

"There aren't any clowns, Cyril." Greg had to assure Cyril there wouldn't be any clowns in the abandoned restaurant in order to convince Cyril to come along. Not that Greg knew one way or the other.

"What's that one?" Cyril pointed at a large-headed figure with a big nose. It sat under a sign that read, TOP PRIZE.

Greg picked it up before Hadi could. It was heavy, and its fur felt matted and coarse. He was oddly drawn to the animal, whatever it was. He studied the pointed ears, sloped forehead, long snout, and piercing yellow eyes. Then he noticed the blue collar around the animal's neck. Something gleaming dangled from the collar. A dog tag? He lifted it.

"Fetch," Hadi read over Greg's shoulder. "It's a dog, named Fetch."

Greg loved dogs for the most part, but he hoped to never see one like this one in real life. He held the dog up and turned it this way and that.

Even the vicious old dog that lived next door to Greg wasn't this ugly. Fetch looked like someone had crossed the big bad wolf with the shark from *Jaws*. His (surely it was a he?) head was a triangle, pointy on top and with a mouth far too wide for comfort at the bottom. Fetch's fur, which looked grayish brown in the splotchy glow of their flashlights, was missing in places, revealing tarnished metal beneath. A couple of wires stuck out of the big ears, and a partially exposed cavity in Fetch's belly revealed what looked like a primitive circuit board.

"Look at this." Cyril was, surprisingly, now interested in the counter. He picked up a small booklet inside a plastic sheath. "I think it's the instructions."

"Let me see." Greg plucked the booklet from Cyril's grasp.

"Hey," Cyril squeaked.

Greg ignored his protests. This could be it.

Putting Fetch back on the counter, he pulled the booklet from the plastic and scanned through the instructions. Hadi read over his shoulder. Cyril stuck his head between Greg's chest and the booklet, forcing Greg to hold the booklet farther out so they could all read together. Fetch, the instructions explained, was an animatronic dog designed to sync up with your phone and retrieve information and other things for you.

"That's lit," Hadi said. "Think it still works?"

"How long has this place been empty?" Greg asked. "Fetch looks like he's older than my dad, but smartphones haven't been around that long."

Hadi shrugged. Greg finally did, too, and he began poking around Fetch to find the control panel. Hadi and Cyril lost interest.

"It isn't going to work. It's older tech; it won't be compatible with our phones," Cyril said, cringing when the wind surged against the building again.

Greg felt a chill slither down his spine. Whether it was related to the wind's eerie onslaught or something else, he wasn't sure.

Greg returned his attention to Fetch. He wanted to see if he could get the dog-thing to do whatever it was supposed to do. He had a hunch this might be what he'd felt in the field, what had called him here.

Cyril's pessimism about Fetch didn't surprise Greg. He wouldn't know an opportunity if it thumped him between the eyes.

Hadi, on the other hand, was relentlessly positive. He had such a sunny disposition he'd pulled off what Greg thought was nothing less than a magic trick: Hadi was accepted by the popular crowd, despite having spent most of his time with Greg and Cyril, two of the nerdiest kids in the school.

Maybe it had something to do with his looks. Greg had heard girls talking about Hadi. Hadi was either "fine," "hot," "cute," "sharp," or just *"mmhmm,"* depending on the girl who was talking.

Hadi wandered away from the counter, and Cyril plopped down in a chair at the nearest table. "I think we should go," he said.

"Nah," Hadi brushed him off. "There's still a lot to check out."

Greg ignored them both. He'd picked up Fetch and found a panel under Fetch's belly. Juggling the instructions, Fetch, and his flashlight, Greg bit his lip and concentrated on hitting the right buttons in the right sequence.

For an instant, the wind and rain let up, leaving the building in a silence that felt almost menacing. Greg glanced up at the ceiling. He noticed a large stain above his head. A water stain? Distracted from his task for a second, he shined his light over the whole ceiling. No other stains. In fact, why wasn't the whole inside of the restaurant dripping? He thought he'd seen part of the metal roof missing when he'd first looked at the building. Why wasn't it leaking?

Shrugging, he returned his attention to Fetch. At this point, he was just randomly pushing buttons. None of the sequences laid out in the instructions were doing anything.

As abruptly as it had stopped, the wind and rain started up again in a crescendo of maniacal drumming, pounding, and wailing. That's when Fetch moved.

Suddenly, with a whirring sound, Fetch's head raised. Then his gaping, tooth-filled mouth opened. And he growled.

"What the hell!" Greg dropped Fetch on the counter and leaped back. Simultaneously, Cyril erupted from his chair.

"What?" Hadi asked, returning to his friends.

Greg pointed at Fetch, whose head and mouth were in clearly different positions than they had been when they'd found him.

"Sick," Hadi said.

They all stared at Fetch, edging backward in unspoken agreement that a little distance was a good idea in case Fetch did something else.

They waited.

So did Fetch.

Hadi got bored first. He shined his flashlight in the direction of the stage. "What do you think is behind that curtain?"

"I think I don't want to know," Cyril said.

Behind them, a door slammed . . . inside the building.

As a unit, the boys ran through the dining room and down the hall to the storage room they'd broken into. Even though he was the smallest, Cyril reached the room first. He was out through the narrow gap they'd managed to create in the jammed service door opening before the other boys could squeeze through.

Outside, pelted by rain streaking sideways, they grabbed

their bikes. Greg figured the wind was gusting over fifty mph now. No way could they bike home. He looked at Hadi, whose curly black hair was matted against his head. Hadi burst out laughing, and Greg joined in. Cyril hesitated, then started laughing, too.

"Come on," Hadi shouted over the screaming wind. Without looking back at the restaurant, they put their heads down and pushed their bikes against the storm.

As he trudged beside his friends, Greg thought about why he'd wanted them to come to the abandoned restaurant. They'd left so much of it unexplored . . . like the area behind the curtain. There'd been three closed doors off the hallway, too. What was behind them? Greg was afraid he might not have gotten what he was there for. Had he done what he was meant to do?

Greg was close to home when a woman called out, "Wet enough for you?"

He stopped, wiped his eyes, and squinted through the rain.

"Hey, Mrs. Peters," he called when he saw his elderly neighbor standing on her covered front porch.

She threw up her skinny arms. "Love these storms!" she sang out.

He laughed and waved at her. "Enjoy!" he shouted.

She waved too, and he plodded on. When he neared his parents' tall, modern, oceanfront house, Greg was surprised to see a light in the living room window. The town was still dark. When he'd parted with Cyril and Hadi, the only lights he'd seen were their flashlights bobbing along like disembodied spirits, and the flickers of what looked like candles inside a couple houses. The light in his window, however, was bright and steady.

When he pulled his bike in next to the stilts that raised the house a full story off the ground, he discovered why he'd seen light. At first drowned out by the thunderous sounds of the wind and rain, he hadn't heard the motor until he practically walked into it. A shiny new generator sat under the house, chugging away, a cord extending past the two-car garage and up the stairs to the front door.

Greg peeled off his dripping rain jacket as he climbed the steps, but before he reached the front door, it opened.

"There you are, boyo!" Greg's uncle Darrin grinned down at him, his mountainous six-foot-five, broad-shouldered frame filling the doorway. "I was about to mount a search posse. You didn't answer your phone."

Greg reached the entry and exchanged his and his uncle's signature greeting—a half-hug-double-fist-bump. "Sorry, Dare. I didn't hear it." He pulled the phone from his pocket and tapped it. Dare had texted and called him multiple times. "Wow. I swear I didn't hear it."

"Who could hear anything in this wind? Get inside."

"Where'd the generator come from?" Greg asked. He didn't really care. He was trying to distract himself from thinking about why he didn't hear his phone in the restaurant.

It hadn't been *that* loud inside. Could it have been because . . .

"I got it in Olympia. Your dad's been saying for years you don't need it, but that's bullhonky. I told him he's going to wish he had one. They've been saying the storms will be much worse this winter. And wouldn't you know it, they came *early* this year. How about that rain we got last week for Halloween?" Dare shook his head. "Of course, your dad won't listen."

Greg didn't remember that argument. But then, Dare and Greg's dad had so many arguments, how could he remember any specific one?

Uncle Darrin was Greg's mother's brother, her only sibling, and they were close; Greg and Dare were even closer. But Greg's dad hated Dare for the very reasons Greg loved him—because Dare was flamboyant and fun.

"Darrin needs to grow up," Greg's dad would say over and over.

With long hair, died purple and worn in a braid, and a wardrobe of bright-colored suits and ties paired with painfully patterned shirts, Dare had his own distinct look. That Dare was also a wealthy, successful inventor of car parts and had the most amazing luck with investments and money in general was the nail in his coffin as far as Greg's dad was concerned. "People like him don't deserve success," he often groused. Greg's dad was a contractor, and he worked more than he wanted to afford their big house and the expensive cars he liked. The fact that Dare lived on a ten-acre estate and made tons of money from "tinkering" in his workshop was "too much."

Greg loved Dare the way he wished he could love his dad. Dare had done nothing but accept Greg from the day his squished little head entered the world, despite the fact that Greg was never a cute baby, and he hadn't turned into a cute kid. His face was too long, his eyes were too close together, and his nose was too small. He compensated for all of that with long, wavy blond hair, a "great smile" (or so a girl in his former eighth-grade class had said), and enough height and muscle to think he might not be a total lost cause after high school. Never drawn to typical boy things like cars and sports—no matter how hard his dad tried to force them down his throat—Greg found an ally in Dare, who didn't question Greg's likes or dislikes. He accepted Greg as he was.

"Where's Mom?" Greg asked Dare.

"Book club."

Greg didn't ask about his dad. One, he didn't care. Two, he knew his dad would be playing poker with his buddies. That was how he spent his Saturday evenings—even if he had to play cards by candlelight.

"Where were you boys in this weather?" Dare asked.

"Um, can I keep that a secret?"

Dare tilted his huge head and stroked his graying goatee. "Sure. I trust you."

"Thanks."

"You want to play backgammon?" Dare asked.

"Can I take a rain check?"

"Ha! Good one." Dare gestured to Greg's still dripping coat.

Greg shook his head. "Unintentional. Um, I just wanted to do some reading?"

"Sure. No prob. I just came by to set up the generator for you guys. When you weren't here and I couldn't get ahold of you, I figured I'd stay until worry fried my circuits and made me phone the police."

Greg grinned. "I'm glad I made it home before you called the cops."

"Me too." Dare started to reach for his magenta raincoat, then hesitated and snapped his fingers. "Oh, by the way, I heard you got your first babysitting gig. Glad you finally brought your old man around."

"It was really thanks to you. Once you threw your two cents in, it was three against one. I'm sitting for the McNallys' kid next week—Jake? They need someone to watch him on Saturdays."

"No way! His mom and I go way back. Maybe I'll stop by sometime, bring you guys a treat . . . or bring by my new puppy. I've been thinking seriously about getting a dog."

"Really? Cool!"

"Yeah, a friend has a Shih Tzu that's going to have puppies soon. I'm thinking I've been without a dog long enough. I miss having a dog to cuddle with."

Greg laughed. "Just be sure it's a *nice* Shih Tzu. I think the beast next door is part Shih Tzu."

"That snaggle-toothed mongrel? Nah, no dog of mine will be like that. Remember," Dare said, holding up his right index finger, on which he wore his favorite onyx and gold ring, "I have . . ."

"The Magic Finger of Luck," Dare and Greg said in unison.

They laughed.

"The Magic Finger of Luck" had been an ongoing joke since Greg was about four years old. One day, Greg was crying because he wanted the stuffed octopus in a claw machine. He hadn't been able to get it when his mother put money in the machine and he'd tried with the claw. Dare had tapped the glass of the claw machine with his right index finger and had said in a deep voice, "I have the Magic Finger of Luck. I will get you the octopus." And he had done it on the first try. After that, Dare called on the Magic Finger of Luck to get things to go his way. It pretty much always worked.

Greg stopped laughing, thinking again about the neighbor's dog.

"Yeah, I still can't believe that thing bit me." The neighbors next door had moved in the year before, and two days later, their dog, a small but evil mutt with very sharp teeth and one missing eye, charged out at Greg and bit him on the ankle. He had to have ten stitches.

"Okay, I'll go and leave you to your reading," Dare said. "Before I go, though, let's make sure everything's working right."

Fifteen minutes later, Greg was lounging on his double bed reading by the nice bright light of his red pendant reading lamp. Dare had gotten the family a power transfer system for the generator that hooked up to the breaker box. With the flip of a few switches, power was restored to the whole house. "Got this especially for your gaming needs," Dare said before giving Greg another half-hug-double-fist-bump and leaving.

Even though he really wanted to get to his reading, Greg took the time to do his nightly yoga routine before sliding under the oversize afghan Dare had knitted for him. Dare had also taught him yoga, and Greg loved it. It not only calmed him down before bed, it helped him stay in shape. Not that "good shape" was good enough.

Greg stood in front of the mirror and examined his narrow shoulders and slight chest. Even though he had muscles in his arms and legs, his torso was still too thin. And his face . . .

Greg's phone buzzed. He picked it up and looked at a text from Hadi.

U recovered?

Greg snorted. As if he was scared enough to need recovering. **From what?** he texted back, playing dumb.

U can't fool me.

OK, Greg responded. Yeah, I'm good. Need more courage I guess.

You need Brian Rhineheart's brain. He's not afraid of anything.

Greg laughed. Good point. Brian Rhineheart was the football team's star running back. He texted, I could use his legs, too. Fast, for running away.

LOL How about Steve Thornton's shoulders? Powerful enough to thump scary things.

Greg laughed again. But Hadi was onto something. If Greg was going to do what he'd set out to do, why didn't he pick and choose what he wanted?

Okay, he typed in, but I want Don Warring's chest, too, then.

Greg grinned at the idea of constructing a body from football players' parts. He needed a good face, though. Especially if he was going to get a girl to pay attention to him.

I want Ron Fisher's eyes, he texted.

RGR. How about Neal Manning's nose?

Greg smiled and typed, OBV.

Mouth?

Greg thought about it. He responded, Zach's.

BFG.

Greg smiled. He could picture Hadi's "big freaking grin."

Hair?

I like my own, Greg replied.

Ego much?

Greg laughed.

GG

Greg typed in, **BFN**.

Greg flopped onto his bed.

He picked up his journal and the book on the Zero Point Field he needed to check. He glanced over at his plants before he started reading. They were the key to this, weren't they? They made the exchange he'd just had with Hadi more than just a silly game. Well, they were at least the catalyst. Learning about Cleve Backster's experiments is what had launched him down the road he was on.

But the plants wouldn't help him tonight. He needed to review what he knew about Random Event Generators, or REGs. He flipped through his book. Yes, there it was. Machines and consciousness. Cause and effect. He put the book down and skimmed his last journal entry.

He hadn't misinterpreted what he'd gotten, had he? No. He didn't think so. He was either on the right track, or he wasn't. And if he wasn't, he didn't think he wanted to know what track he was on. The way he'd been drawn to that place couldn't have been a coincidence.

The storm hung around another day, but it fizzled out late Sunday night. Power came back on. School was in session as usual Monday morning.

Greg endured the first half of the day and was relieved when

1:10 p.m. finally rolled around and he got to go to Advanced Scientific Theory. Advanced Scientific Theory was an AP class reserved for freshmen who had won science fair prizes in the previous two years. The class had only twelve students. It was taught by a visiting teacher, Mr. Jacoby, who also taught at Grays Harbor Community College.

As always, Greg was the first one in the classroom. He sat in the front. Only Hadi would sit near him.

Mr. Jacoby was practically bouncing at the front of the yellow-walled classroom when the bell rang. Tall and lanky but so full of energy he reminded Greg of a long, coiled spring, Mr. Jacoby was an enthusiastic teacher who was undaunted by disinterested students. Greg loved science, all science, not just tech, and his passion had earned him the title of teacher's pet.

Mr. Jacoby always lectured while darting around the front of the classroom like he had bugs in his pants. Sometimes he scribbled on the whiteboard. More often, he just rambled. But it was interesting stuff. This small room, filled with tall wooden lab tables and counter-height chairs, was one of Greg's favorite places in the school. He loved the Periodic Table and the constellation posters on the walls. He loved the smell of the fertilizer that fed the hybrid plants growing at the back of the room, it made him think of science and learning.

Running a hand through unruly red hair, Mr. Jacoby began, "In quantum physics, there is something known as the Zero Point Field. This field is scientific proof that there is no such thing as a vacuum, no such thing as nothingness. If you empty all space of matter and energy, you still find, in subatomic terms, a bunch of activity. This constant activity is a field of energy that is always in motion, subatomic matter constantly interacting with other subatomic matter." Mr. Jacoby rubbed a freckled nose. "Are you all with me?"

Greg nodded enthusiastically. Hadi, who sat next to him at the three-person lab table, nudged him. "Hey, this is your shtick."

Greg ignored him.

Mr. Jacoby grinned at Greg and took his nod to represent the entire class, which was unwise, but Greg was fine with it.

"Good," Mr. Jacoby continued. "So this energy is called the Zero Point Field because fluctuations in the field are still found in temperatures of absolute zero. Absolute zero is the lowest possible energy state, where everything's been removed and there should be nothing remaining to make any motion. Make sense?"

Greg nodded again.

"Great. So the energy should be zero, but when they measure the energy, mathematically, it never actually reaches zero. There's always some remaining vibration due to continued particle exchange. Still with me?"

Greg nodded enthusiastically. He'd had no idea Mr. Jacoby was going to talk about this today. What were the odds? He grinned. There were no *odds*. It was the field. He was so excited that he missed the next few minutes of Mr. Jacoby's lecture. It didn't matter. He knew this stuff.

He did tune back in, though, when Kimberly Bergstrom raised her hand. Well, he sort of tuned back in. He heard her question: "Is this just theory?"

He also heard the start of Mr. Jacoby's answer. "Not entirely. Consider the scientific trend. Before the scientific revolution . . ."

That's where Greg tuned out again. He got caught up in watching Kimberly. Who wouldn't? Long inky black hair. Amazing green eyes. Prettier than any model Greg had ever seen.

Greg felt himself flush, and he whipped his gaze away from Kimberly before someone caught him staring.

Too late.

Hadi nudged him again, and when Greg looked over, Hadi made goofy goo-goo eyes at him. Greg shifted his attention back to Mr. Jacoby.

As usual, Greg was the last one out of the room when class was over. Mr. Jacoby smiled at him as Greg gathered his stuff, and Greg gave another thought to talking to his teacher. Then he felt his phone vibrate. Waving at Mr. Jacoby, Greg pulled out his phone as he stepped into the hallway. He looked at the screen.

> Hello, Greg. HRU.

The phone number wasn't familiar. Greg looked around. Who was texting him? He entered: **I'm fine. Who's this?** Then he watched his screen.

> Fetch.

"Oh very funny, Hadi," Greg muttered. He texted what he said.

The reply wasn't what he expected:

?4U.

What's your question? Greg texted.

> Why'd U leave?

Greg rolled his eyes and entered, **You're hilarious.**

> TY. U answer.

Greg felt a tap on the shoulder. "You're going to be late for Spanish, amigo," Hadi said.

Greg whipped around. Hadi raised an eyebrow. And Cyril, who stood next to him, took a stutter step back.

"Why are you texting me if you're right here?" Greg asked Hadi.

"Dude, you wacked? Do I look like I'm texting you?"

Uh, actually, no. Hadi's phone was nowhere in sight.

Greg looked back at his phone. Whoever was texting him had repeated:

> U answer.

Greg looked at Cyril. "Did you text me?"

"*No. Por qué habría?*"

"I don't know why you'd text me. And stop speaking in Spanish," Greg said.

Cyril ignored him. "*Venga.*" He tugged on Greg's sleeve.

"I hate Spanish," Greg said.

Cyril looked past Greg and said, "*Hola, Manuel.*"

Greg turned to look at Manuel Gomez, who had transferred into the school a couple weeks before from Madrid, Spain.

"*Hola, Cyril. ¿Como estas?*"

"*Estoy bien. ¿Tú?*"

"*Bueno.*"

"*Oye, Manuel, ¿conoces a Greg?*" Cyril asked, gesturing at Greg.

"*No.*" Manuel smiled at Greg and held out his hand. "*Encantada de conocerte.*"

"He just said, 'Nice to meet you,'" Cyril told Greg.

"*Lo sé,*" Greg said. "I'm not a total Spanish spaz."

"Close enough," Cyril said.

Manuel laughed.

"Greg tiene muchos problemas con el español," Cyril told Manuel.

"I'd be happy to help you with Spanish anytime," Manuel said to Greg. "Want me to give you my number?" He held up his phone.

"Sure." Greg swapped phones with Manuel, and they exchanged numbers.

"Yo, Mousie," someone called out to Cyril. "How's your mom doing? She still a freak like you?"

Greg turned and faced Cyril's bully. He cleared his throat and said loudly, "Remember this, Trent. 'Three things in life are important. The first is to be kind. The second is to be kind. And the third is to be kind.' So said Henry James."

Trent shoved Greg. "You're a freak."

As Trent sauntered away, Hadi nudged Greg. "You read too much."

"You don't read enough."

In unison, they said in exaggerated deep voices, "The universe in balance." They bumped fists and finished with, "Cha!"

A couple of kids in the hall deliberately jostled Greg, and one of them said, "You guys are weird."

"And proud of it," Greg sang.

Hadi shook his head.

Manuel touched Greg's shoulder. "I like Henry James, too." He grinned and held out a fist.

Greg bumped fists with Manuel; then, shoving his phone in his pocket, Greg followed Cyril and Hadi to Spanish.

He wasn't going to talk to them about the texts now. But he didn't stop thinking about the texts, either. If neither Hadi nor Cyril sent them, who did? Was someone else in the restaurant with the boys on Saturday night? Is that what that slamming door was? Or did someone see them leave, then go in and find Fetch?

The idea that they'd been watched made Greg's skin crawl. But the idea that they *hadn't* been watched made all the hairs stand up on Greg's arms. Could it be? He wouldn't think about it. Not yet.

By the next day, he was thinking about it. Hard. In that time, he'd received a dozen texts from Fetch. By now, he realized the texts *had* to be from the animatronic. They couldn't be from anyone else because no one else could know everything Fetch was texting about. Obviously, Fetch was dialed into Greg, so to speak. It quickly became clear that Fetch was synced with Greg's phone, and he was trying to live up to his name. When Greg told Cyril he needed more time to do some homework, Fetch sent Greg a link to a time-management article, and a clock app appeared on Greg's phone. When Greg looked up REGs online, he received a link, from Fetch, to an article about the latest research into intention and REGs. When Greg finished the article, Fetch texted:

> 01001111 01101011 01100001 01111001 00111111.

This baffled Greg until he thought about the article he'd just read. The article talked about the experiments being done that used REGs to measure whether a person could think hard enough to have an effect on an outcome in the physical world. Greg knew REGs generated random 1s and 0s. *Ones and zeros*, Greg thought. Was it possible?

Greg copied Fetch's text into a binary-to-text converter, and sure enough, Fetch had texted, "Okay?" in binary code.

Greg shivered as he texted back, **OK**. He wasn't sure it was okay at all. It was more spooky than okay.

Then things got stranger . . . as if getting texts from an old animatronic dog wasn't bizarre to begin with.

One day, Greg told his mom on the phone that he was craving chocolate. She said what she always said when he mentioned candy. "Not good for you. Have an apple." Later that day, when she got home from shopping, she pulled a chocolate bar out of the bag.

"How'd this get here?" she said in annoyance, tucking her chin-length blonde hair behind an ear. "I didn't buy this." She checked her receipt and discovered the bar was on the order she'd placed online.

"Must be a glitch," she said. "I'll have to email them." When she caught Greg watching her, she said, "Well, it's your lucky day," and tossed him the bar.

As he caught the candy bar, he was pretty sure he couldn't eat it yet. He was too excited. If he was right, Fetch had just fetched him a candy bar.

What else could the animatronic dog do?

And how was he doing it?

Greg could accept, barely, that Fetch was synced with his phone. But Fetch wasn't synced with his mom's phone, was he?

The text messages continued day after day. Sometimes Greg responded, just because. Sometimes not. Either way, he kept a log in his journal. This was giving him important feedback for his project.

A lot of his exchanges with Fetch made no sense. Like the day Fetch texted:

DDAS

Why would I do anything stupid? Greg responded.

Dunno.

Sometimes, the texts were clear. One day, Greg texted Cyril that he was having trouble with the Spanish homework, and he needed the translation for "I don't know how to make banana bread without eggs or flour." Cyril didn't respond, but Fetch texted:

No sé cómo hacer pan de plátano sin huevos ni harina.

Cyril didn't text back until late in the evening. When he did, his translation was the same as Fetch's.

Was it time for Greg to tell his friends what was going on?

He decided to wait.

But then came the spider.

★ ★ ★

One Saturday, a couple weeks before Christmas, Greg was home taking care of Jake, his now usual Saturday babysitting gig. Dare—or "Uncle Dare" to both Greg *and* Jake thanks to Dare's close friendship with Mrs. McNally—had suggested he come over with "a rainy day picnic," complete with a yellow smiley face picnic blanket, some potted plants, rubber toy insects, and a wicker basket full of creative sandwiches like artichoke salad with provolone and raisins on pumpernickel and chicken and peanut butter on rye. Fortunately, Dare knew Greg wasn't as adventurous with food as he was, so he included a couple of ordinary tuna salad sandwiches, too. They set up their picnic in the living room, in front of the big picture window overlooking the dunes and the ocean. You could barely see the ocean through the rain—one shade of gray merged with the next.

Jake, four years old, loved the picnic, but he wasn't keen on the huge rubber spider that lurked near the edge of the picnic blanket. He was so agitated that Greg suggested they put the picnic on hold. He got out two spatulas and made a big production of scooping up the spider and putting it in a sealed plastic bag. That wasn't enough for Jake.

"Out!" he demanded, pointing a chubby finger toward the door.

So Greg put on his rain jacket and went out in the rain. While Dare and Jake supervised from under the shelter of the house, Greg dug a hole in the mud and buried the rubber spider.

Satisfied, Jake ate the rest of his picnic lunch without comment.

"Good job, boyo," Dare said.

Greg enjoyed the praise. He sure never got any from his dad, who, as usual, was working. When Dare was around, though, he didn't seem to mind his father's disapproval as much. His uncle made everything seem better.

A couple days before Christmas, Greg and Hadi were talking on the phone about Trent. "He's such a jerk," Greg said. He laid on his bed watching his plants, sending specific thoughts to them like one might send to an REG. Just like in Cleve Backster's experiments, his plants seemed to be responding well to his latest intentions.

"I don't really pay attention to him," Hadi said, "but I know he freaks out Cyril."

"Yeah."

"He needs to be pranked," Hadi said. "I was thinking spiders. I overheard him the other day telling Zach he's afraid of spiders."

Greg laughed. "Seriously? I've got a rubber one buried in my backyard. Maybe if the rain stops, I'll dig it up before I come over."

"Yeah, do that. Ho, ho, ho. It'd make a nice surprise in his stocking."

Greg waited a few hours, but the rain didn't let up. It thrummed relentlessly on the roof. If Greg hadn't promised

Hadi he'd go over to wrap presents, he wouldn't have left the house.

But he promised, so he geared up for the rain and stepped outside.

He almost screamed when he looked down and saw a huge spider covering the WEL of WELCOME FRIENDS on his mother's jute doormat. Jumping back, he stared at the spider, realizing now what it was.

Greg felt his pulse accelerate.

This. Was. Not. Possible.

But there it was. It was the rubber spider he'd buried— still in its now muddy plastic bag.

No one except Dare and Jake knew where that spider was. Jake and his family had gone to Hawaii for Christmas, and Dare was on a ski trip with friends. "Wish you could be here for our white Christmas, boyo," Dare had said on the phone the night before.

Leaning over and picking up the plastic bag by the corner, as if it was a deadly creature in and of itself, Greg held the bag in front of his face.

Were those teeth marks along the bottom edge?

He dropped the bag.

His phone buzzed. He sucked in his breath and fumbled for his phone.

Merry Xmas.

Merry Christmas to you, too, Fetch, Greg entered while trying to ignore the fact that his fingers were trembling.

He didn't wait for a reply. Ignoring the urge to throw the phone into the shrubs at the edge of his yard, he shoved it back in his pocket. It was time. He had to talk to his friends.

The day after Christmas, the boys gathered in Greg's room, on the bed. Greg sat with his back against the navy blue cushioned headboard, his friends sprawled next to each other at the foot. He glanced around the room, taking comfort in his familiar surroundings. Posters of movie musicals alternated with puppy posters on the walls, and two shelving units stuffed with books flanked the window that looked out toward the ocean. The sky outside was matte gray, as if an artist with no sense of depth had just slathered paint across the horizon. On the wall opposite the window, his plants sat in rows on shelving under a low-hanging bank of grow lights. His antique rolltop desk, a gift from Dare, sat next to the door. A plate of gingerbread cookies Greg had baked two days before sat in the middle of the bed.

Grabbing a cookie, Hadi asked, "What's this urgent meeting about?"

"Yeah," Cyril squeaked. "I was going to go to the day-after Christmas sales with my mom."

Hadi shook his head. "Seriously, dude. Do you listen to yourself? You might as well wear a T-shirt that says, 'Make fun of me.'"

Greg threw a dirty sock at Hadi. "Leave him alone. If he likes to shop with his mom, he likes to shop with his mom."

Hadi gave Greg a mock bow. "You make a point." He nodded toward Cyril, this time for real. "Sorry."

"S'okay."

In the silence that followed, Greg weighed how he was going to explain everything. Well, maybe he wasn't going to explain *everything*. Maybe just some things. For sure he had to tell them about Fetch.

He looked over to his nightstand, which held stacks of books, papers, and his phone, still receiving texts from Fetch. His most recent, an hour before Cyril and Hadi showed up, was:

Do U need food 4 meeting?

No, thank you, Greg texted back.

He took a deep breath and wrinkled his nose at the scent of the lavender air freshener his mother had put someplace in his room. (He'd been looking for it but hadn't found it yet. He preferred the smell of his sweaty clothes, thank you very much.) "Okay, so there's no way to say this but to say it," he began.

Hadi and Cyril looked at him.

"Fetch has been sending me texts."

His friends stared at him. They blinked in unison.

"Who's Fetch?" Hadi asked.

"Wait—you mean that dog thing? That prize fr-from the pizzeria? Is this a joke?" Cyril asked.

Greg shook his head. He picked up one of the stacks of papers from his nightstand—all the text messages he'd printed out—and held it out to Cyril. "Look."

He waited while Cyril and Hadi scooted together so they could read the texts at the same time.

"This can't be real," Cyril said. His voice was even higher than normal.

Hadi grabbed the stack of printouts and flipped through them. He glanced at Greg then said to Cyril, "He wouldn't prank us like that."

"No, I wouldn't," Greg said. "Want to see my phone? I'm smart, but I'm not smart enough to spoof texts on my phone."

Hadi shook his head. He abruptly stood and started pacing in a tiny circle on Greg's blue-and-maroon braided rug.

"It must have synced with your phone, dude," Hadi said finally.

Greg nodded. "Yeah, except—"

"Whoa, wait," Cyril said. "I'm not a techie, but I don't see how something as old as that animatronic dog could sync up with a modern smartphone. That's just not possible."

"Obviously, it is, though," Hadi said.

"It's not just syncing." Greg reached for the muddy plastic bag containing the spider and held it up. He felt like he should say, "Exhibit A," but didn't.

"What's that?" Cyril shifted away so fast he fell off the bed with a thud.

Greg suppressed a laugh while Cyril jumped up.

"Sorry," Greg said. "It's not real." He told them the story of the picnic and then the appearance of the unearthed bag on his doorstep.

Cyril gaped at him, then looked from Hadi to Greg and back to Hadi. "No way."

"Let me see that." Hadi snatched the bag from Greg's grasp and examined it. "Those are teeth marks!"

"No way," Cyril repeated.

"Way," Hadi said.

"It's like my plants, I think," Greg began. It was time to share what he was sure was behind all of this.

Hadi and Cyril stared at him. "What?" Hadi asked.

"Have you heard of Cleve Backster?" Greg asked, pretty sure they hadn't.

They shook their heads.

"He was a polygraph expert who started doing experiments with plants in the 1960s."

"Okay," Hadi said. "So what?"

"So, in the 1960s, Backster had the idea to hook up a plant to a polygraph machine to see if he could measure how long osmosis took. Although he didn't learn a thing about osmosis, he stumbled upon something else, something super cool." Greg stopped.

Cyril and Hadi were still staring at the spider in the bag. They probably weren't even listening to him, and even if they were, Greg realized there was no way he was ready to tell them his theory.

"What if someone was in the building with us and now they're watching you?" Cyril asked, confirming that he and Hadi hadn't been listening.

"What? Like a stalker?" Hadi asked.

"And he bugged my phone or something?" Greg asked. "That's just crazy."

But was it any crazier than what he thought was going on?

Greg's phone buzzed. He picked it up and read the incoming text. He dropped the phone on the bed.

Hadi and Cyril looked from the phone to Greg.

He pointed at it. When they leaned over to look at it, he looked, too, and read the text again:

EL.

"What's EL?" Cyril asked.

Hadi went pale. He met Greg's wide-eyed gaze.

"Evil laugh," they said in unison.

An animatronic dog that wanted to be helpful was one thing. An animatronic dog that wanted to be helpful and had a sense of humor was okay. But an animatronic dog who had an agenda . . . that was, well, scary.

After that, Greg stopped trying to get Hadi and Cyril to understand what he thought was going on with Fetch. So when they finished freaking out about Fetch's text, he told them he'd keep them posted and decided it was time to conduct more experiments.

Going to the abandoned restaurant in itself had been a test, and he still wasn't sure how that had turned out. It had started with him putting an intention out, a desire backed by his will that it unfold. That had led to an impulse to act. The impulse had taken him to the restaurant, where he found Fetch. But how did Fetch play into the grand scheme of things?

He had to figure it out.

He decided to start with something small and specific.

The next day, he got his first experiment's result. In Advanced Scientific Theory, Mr. Jacoby, looking even more nerdy than usual in a blue checked short-sleeved shirt under a red-and-blue argyle sweater vest, started his lecture with, "So now that we understand the Zero Point Field, let's see if we can figure out what it means for the real world. To this end, we're going to talk about REGs."

Awesome! Greg thought.

"A random event generator, usually referred to as an REG," Mr. Jacoby said, "is a machine that basically flips a coin. Not really, of course. But it's a machine that's designed to generate a random output, just the same as you'd get by flipping a coin, assuming you're not cheating at it." Mr. Jacoby grinned then continued. "Instead of heads or tails, REGs produce a positive or negative pulse and then turn the pulses into ones and zeros, which as you know is binary code, the language of computers. Once the pulses are in binary code, they can be stored and counted. Researchers built the REGs as a way of studying the impact that focused thought has on events. Make sense?"

Greg nodded, and he noticed Kimberly did as well.

"Excellent." Mr. Jacoby clapped his hands once. "So I

was able to get a small REG, and now it's time to do some intention experiments with it. I'm assigning partners."

Greg held his breath. *Will it work?*

He only had to wait through two pairings to find out. "Greg and Kimberly," Mr. Jacoby said, "Pair up."

Kimberly turned gracefully in her chair, her hair sweeping through the air like she was in a shampoo commercial. She smiled at Greg, and his bones nearly disintegrated. He had to clutch the lab table to stay in his seat.

His intention had worked.

Grinning back at Kimberly and waving at her so exuberantly that her own smile faltered a little, Greg forced himself to stay seated. He had enough wits about him to know that if he did a happy dance, he'd be laughed at for years.

Mr. Jacoby made everyone move around so partners were seated together. He instructed them to exchange phone numbers because they'd need to stay in contact. Greg had to concentrate to keep his hand steady when he passed his phone to Kimberly and took her phone, tucked into a bright purple case, to enter his number. After they returned each other's phones and Mr. Jacoby started explaining the experiment's instructions, Greg's phone buzzed, and per class rules, he ignored it. It wasn't until he was out in the hall, after he and Kimberly set a time to meet to do the first step of the experiment, that he checked his phone. Fetch had texted.

Congrats.

* * *

At the end of the day, Greg couldn't wait to get home to record the triumph in his journal. Unfortunately, he'd missed the bus that morning, and he'd had to bike to school. That wasn't a problem, but now the wind was blowing from the southeast, and he couldn't bike hard enough to overcome the gusts trying to shove him back toward the school. Eventually he gave up and walked his bike the rest of the way to his house. He was so lost in thought he forgot about the tiny terror that lived next door.

It was like a rabid furry missile was careening toward him at top speed. He nearly jumped to Mars when the dog launched itself from an outdoor table and threw itself over the fence right at him.

"Crap!" He let go of his bike and dropped his backpack, catching the dog just as it hit his chest and started snapping at his jugular. What *was* it with this dog? On reflex, he pushed the dog back over the short fence.

When the dog hit the ground, it came up barking and snarling, and it flung itself against the wooden boards. Greg didn't wait to see what it would do next. He grabbed his bike and backpack and ran for his house. Once inside, he realized he was hyperventilating. Sinking to the floor in the puddle created by his dripping coat, he texted Hadi, **Devil Dog just tried to slash my throat. Scared the hell out of me.**

U OK? Hadi responded.

Shaken, not stirred.

Hadi texted back, **LOL.**

★   ★   ★

That night, Greg had nightmares. Not a surprise. He spent the whole night in the abandoned pizzeria being chased alternately by Fetch, a faceless man, and the dog next door while plants grew so fast inside the restaurant that the place turned into a jungle. On the stage, an REG spewed out 0s and 1s almost too fast for the eye to register.

Greg woke up covered in sweat. Did the dream mean it was working . . . or not?

Shaking off the bad night, Greg scowled out the window at the sideways rain. More wind? Apparently Dare was right about this year's winter storms.

He threw on some clothes quickly, already late for school. Racing to the door, Greg waved at his mom, who was on the phone. He ignored his dad, who was scowling at a spreadsheet on his laptop while he guzzled coffee.

Greg threw on his rain jacket, grabbed his backpack, and went out the door and down the steps. That's where he came to a stop so abrupt, he lost his balance and had to grab the stair railing.

His eyes widened. His pulse rate flew into overdrive, and his stomach clenched.

This couldn't be happening.

Turning away from what was in front of him, Greg staggered to the nearest bush and threw up. All he had in his stomach was water, which came up, along with yellow bile. Then, even though his stomach was empty, it lurched some more and he endured a couple rounds of dry heaves.

Finally, he collapsed onto the bottom step of the stairs and wiped his mouth. His fingers were stiff and cold.

He took several deep breaths, cringing at the sour smell of his vomit and the stench coming from next to his bike. Greg stood. He didn't want to stand, and his legs felt so weak it was clear they weren't on board with the idea, either, but he had to do something before his parents came out.

Looking around wildly, as if someone might appear to help him—which actually was the last thing he wanted—he tried to figure out what to do. Well, he knew what he had to do. He had to move it. Which meant he had to touch it.

No way was he going to touch it.

He smacked himself on the forehead. "Think, dummy!"

The admonition worked. He dug his keys out of his pocket and strode to the garden shed tucked against the back of his house. Dropping his keys twice before he could get the right one in the lock, he was drenched by the time he stepped inside the shed and retrieved the black plastic garbage bag he was after.

Now that he was in action, he moved at hyperspeed. He slammed and locked the shed door, not worrying about the sound because the wind and rain drowned out everything. He raced back to his bike.

And once again, he had to confront what he didn't want to look at. This time, he made himself look, really look.

The neighbor's dog lay, dead, against the back wheel of

Greg's bike tire. Its throat torn apart, its belly gutted, intestines flopping onto the concrete. It was stiff, and its eyes were wide open, as if staring in fear, maybe for the first . . . and last . . . time of its life. Greg forced himself to examine the dog's fatal wounds. Yeah. It's just what his subconscious mind told him in his first glance. The dog hadn't been killed with a knife or some other sharp object. It had been ferociously ripped by teeth and claws. It had been attacked by another animal.

Greg gagged and swallowed down another dry heave. Breathing through his mouth, he opened the plastic bag and put it down over the dog. Once he had it covered, he slipped the bag under the animal and used the plastic to scoop up the entrails. When he had it all, he carried the bag to the bushes between his and his neighbor's house and emptied it into the bushes. The dog fell with a sickening *splat* onto the ground.

Greg looked up at his house to be sure neither of his parents were looking out the window. Nope. All good. The neighbor's house was one story. They couldn't see into his yard, and this part of the yard was sheltered from the street. No one was watching him. Even so, this probably wasn't the best plan in the world.

But it was the best he had.

If the dog was a human, forensics would point to Greg in a nanosecond. But the corpse was a dog. He didn't figure there'd be much of an investigation when the body was found. It looked like the nasty little thing had been mauled by a coyote.

But it hadn't been.

As much as he'd love to convince himself that's what happened, Greg knew no coyote would kill a dog and then pose it next to Greg's bike. Because the dog had clearly been posed. Although a little blood from the dog's neck and intestines stained the concrete next to Greg's tire, it wasn't nearly enough blood for the savagery of the dog's wounds. The dog must have been killed someplace else.

No, coyotes had nothing to do with the dog's death.

Greg realized he was frozen in place by the bush. He wadded up the plastic bag, trotted to the trash bin under his house, and stuffed it inside one of the bags of kitchen trash. He closed the lid.

That's when his phone buzzed.

He didn't want to look at it.

But he had to. The incoming text was, as Greg knew it would be, from Fetch:

YW.

Greg was still staring at the screen when another text came in, this one from Hadi: WRU?

He should have been at Hadi's house to catch the bus there five minutes ago. He quickly texted, SRY. L8.

Then he grabbed his bike and pedaled out into the rain, hoping that the wind at his back would help him get to Hadi's before the bus arrived.

★ ★ ★

Greg spent the day paying very little attention to what was going on around him. Every chance he got, he pulled out his phone and scrolled back to delete old text messages.

The spider had spooked him. But the dead dog had terrified him . . . Fetch had *killed* the dog to help Greg. What other "help" would Fetch try to offer? It didn't take long after finding the dog for Greg to conclude that Fetch could do all kinds of nasty things with what Greg had said he wanted. So he tried to find any text in which he'd suggested he wanted or needed anything.

But the problem was, Fetch seemed to be doing more than accessing old messages or conversations. Fetch seemed to be listening in to Greg's life. *How?*

Greg needed to talk to Hadi and Cyril. He needed their help.

Unfortunately, two days passed before he was able to convince Hadi and Cyril to help him do what he knew he needed to do. He wasn't able to tell them about the neighbor's dog until after school. Predictably, they were freaked. Cyril wanted to forget it as soon as he heard it. Hadi, though, wanted to see "the stiff." So he followed Greg home, and they stood together in the rain staring at the dead dog, which was now a wet, grisly pile of viscera and fur.

"I want to go back to the restaurant," Greg told Hadi once they were up in Greg's room.

Hadi stared at him. "After that," he waved a hand in the direction of where the dead dog lay, "you want to go back?"

"Well, *want* is probably not the right word. But I need to. I have to know what's going on."

Hadi shook his head and said he was going home.

But Greg was persistent. He hounded Hadi and Cyril relentlessly via text that evening and in person the next morning and on the phone the next afternoon until he convinced them to return to the restaurant with him. After school, they huddled together in the school lobby before racing through the rain to their bus.

"It will still be raining tonight," Greg told them. "Fewer people out."

"Yeah. Whatever," Hadi said.

"We're going to die," Cyril said.

Greg laughed. "We're not going to die."

So why was his stomach doing somersaults, and why had his heart relocated to his throat?

It was a little harder to get away from their families on a Wednesday night, but they managed it by saying they were going to do homework together at Greg's house. His parents, per usual, were out. His mom had taken a part-time job as a front desk clerk at one of the hotels. He wasn't sure what that was about, and he didn't ask. His dad was working late on his most recent build. "I hate the finishing work," he'd complained that morning. "That's when the client always gets nitpicky."

The first time they'd gone to the restaurant, Greg and his friends had been armed only with a crowbar and flashlights. This time, they also each brought along kitchen knives, and Hadi stuck his baseball bat in his backpack.

It was just as easy to break into the restaurant the second time . . . actually, even easier. The service door lock they'd broken hadn't been repaired or replaced. They just had to pull the heavy door open and slip through.

Once inside, they flipped on their flashlights and shined them around. They started with the ground. Clearly, they all had the same idea. They were looking for footprints other than theirs in the dust covering the cracked blue linoleum floor. Unfortunately, they'd scuffed up the dust so much on their first trip it was impossible to tell for sure whether anyone else had been here.

"Do we have a plan?" Cyril asked when they moved out into the hallway.

Greg noticed all three of them were breathing fast. His voice sounded breathless when he said, "I think we should start by finding Fetch."

They walked shoulder to shoulder along the hallway. It was much quieter in the building this time because the rain, although steady, was soft. It was foggy, too. That tended to dampen sounds.

"So, I found out something about the restaurant," Cyril

said. His voice sounded too loud and too forced.

"What?" Hadi asked.

"This was part of a pizza chain that . . . closed down after something happened at one of them."

"What happened?" Greg asked.

"I don't know. It took a lot of time to even find what I found. I just found a reference to it on a message board for people who like to explore abandoned places."

Hadi came to a dead stop, his flashlight beam jittering out onto the floor in front of him.

"What?" Cyril asked.

Greg looked along the illuminated shaft of Hadi's light.

Cyril squealed.

Greg couldn't blame him.

Dog tracks came out of the pizzeria's eating area and headed toward the lobby.

"What the—?" Hadi still hadn't budged.

"You did turn it on," Cyril said to Greg.

"Yeah, way to go, dude," Hadi said.

Before Greg could respond, a clatter and crash came from inside one of the closed doorways along the hall.

Cyril squealed again. Hadi dropped his flashlight.

"We need to see what's in those rooms," Greg said.

Hadi retrieved his flashlight and shined it in Greg's face. Greg squeezed his eyes shut and turned away.

"Are you out of your mind?" Hadi asked.

"Probably. But I have to know what's going on. I'm going

to check it out. You don't have to if you don't want to."

"I don't want to," Cyril said.

"Fine." Greg dug the crowbar out of his backpack, looked at the knife, and concluded that he didn't have enough hands to hold a crowbar, a knife, and his flashlight. So he got a firm grip on both crowbar and flashlight then took five steps toward the nearest closed door. He noticed a small sign he'd missed the last time. It read CONTROL ROOM.

He stuck the crowbar under his arm and reached for the doorknob.

Hadi appeared at his side. "Can't let you go in there alone, dude." He produced the baseball bat from his backpack and gripped it hard.

Cyril scurried over. "I'm not waiting out here by myself!"

"Thanks," Greg said.

He turned the knob, took a breath, and threw the door open. He quickly re-armed himself with the crowbar.

All three flashlight beams sliced through the dusty blackness and revealed a bank of old computer monitors, keyboards, and what looked like control panels filled with dials and knobs. Nothing else was in the room.

"I don't see anything that could have made that sound," Hadi said.

Greg nodded. "Let's try the next room."

"Wait." Hadi crossed to the nearest keyboard and tapped keys. He turned a couple dials on the control panels. Nothing happened. He shrugged. "Had to check."

Cyril, gaining courage from his friend, came farther into the room and tapped and pushed buttons, too. Still nothing happened.

Greg left the room and headed to the next closed door. As he figured they would, his friends followed.

This door was marked SECURITY and the room behind it was similar to the first one. More dated computer monitors looked back at the boys blankly. Nothing worked.

One last closed door. This one was labeled STORAGE.

"The sound must have come from in here," Greg said. He reached for the knob. But Cyril grabbed his arm. "Wait!"

Greg looked at Cyril.

"You never told us what you wanted to do here. Why are we here?"

"Yeah, dude," Hadi agreed. "You kept saying you had to 'see.' See what? Fetch? What are you going to do when you see him? Interrogate him? Reason with him? He's a piece of machinery."

"Yeah," Cyril said, "and when we left him, he wasn't in there." He pointed to the door.

Greg didn't know how to explain why he needed to be here. "I have to know whether someone else was here and is pranking us. And if it's Fetch, I want to see how it's working."

He didn't bother explaining why he had to look in this room. Before they could protest again, he opened the door.

And he fell back into his friends. Cyril screamed. Hadi gasped.

Staring back at the boys, in the gleaming streams of their lights, were four life-size animatronic characters. They were at least five times bigger than Fetch, who was about the size of a beagle.

Greg recovered himself first. He aimed his light around the room. Every time the beam landed on something, Greg's breath caught. The room didn't just house the four characters. It was also filled with animatronic parts and character costumes, a whole wardrobe full of them.

Dozens of pairs of sightless eyes stared at them through the flashlight-transected gloom. Or at least Greg hoped they were sightless.

His friends hadn't spoken since they opened the door. Suddenly, a raspy humming sound filled the room. The boys' lights skittered all over the space, searching for the sound's origin.

One of the animatronic characters seemed to move its leg, and then something small, dark, and furry shot out from behind it, arced toward the boys, barked, and then bolted out of the room. Before they could do more than gasp in unison, whatever it was disappeared from view.

Cyril shrieked and tore from the room. Greg and Hadi were at his heels.

This wasn't a thinking moment.

That was Fetch that had leaped out at them, wasn't it?

Had to be.

Even though Hadi or Greg could have hit Fetch, or

whatever that thing was, with the baseball bat or crowbar, Greg's brain didn't even consider that. Apparently Hadi's didn't, either. They had just one conscious idea in their heads: *run*.

As they dashed down the hallway toward their exit, Greg tried not to hear the growling and claw-tapping that followed them. He also firmly closed the door on his mind when it tried to ask questions about how Fetch . . . *No! Not going there.*

Get out, get out, get out. That was the only agenda.

It took them only seconds to reach the door and squeeze through it, Cyril in the lead and Greg bringing up the rear. Was that a nip at his heel right before he pulled his foot through and shut the door?

Not going there, either.

Without speaking, the boys grabbed their bikes, but just as they did, a whine behind them made them pause. With a shaking hand, Greg aimed his flashlight at the pizzeria.

A wet, stray mutt trotted toward them, but when Cyril yelped in fear, the dog veered away into the fir trees that surrounded the abandoned building.

"It wasn't Fetch." Greg let go of his bike.

"I don't care," Cyril said.

"I do," Greg said. "I want to find Fetch and figure out what he's doing. I'm going back in."

"I'm going home," Cyril said.

Hadi looked from Greg to Cyril and back again. Greg shrugged—albeit a little shakily—and headed toward the pizzeria.

"You can't go in there alone." Hadi let go of his bike, too, and followed Greg. He looked at Cyril. "The real dog made that noise we heard and probably the tracks, too."

Cyril hugged himself then sighed. "If I die, I'm going to come back and kill you both."

"That's fair," Greg said.

The boys re-entered the pizzeria. They stuck close together as they went down the hall, closing the storage room door as they went past. Without speaking, they made their way to the dining area.

Their flashlight beams zooming this way and that like spotlights, they crossed the room to the prize counter. They only got halfway there before they all paused.

They didn't have to get any closer to see what they came to see.

Fetch was no longer on the counter.

Greg flicked his beam to the floor and then all around the prize counter. No Fetch.

"Maybe he fell behind the counter," Hadi suggested, not sounding particularly convinced of his theory.

"Maybe."

Since neither of his friends moved, Greg took a huge breath and shuffled forward. "Let me know if you see anything," he told his friends.

"We've got your back," Hadi said.

Greg wasn't so sure, but he had to know if Fetch was there. Ignoring the trickle of sweat that ran down between his shoulder blades, Greg reached the counter and started tiptoeing around it.

"Dude," Hadi said, "don't you think he would have heard us by now?"

Greg flinched. Good point. He laughed, but the sound was more of a croak when it came out. So he rushed around the counter and threw his light beam everywhere it could reach.

Fetch wasn't there.

Greg turned and looked at his friends. "Fetch is gone."

"What are you going to do?" Cyril asked.

"I'm . . . not sure," Greg confessed.

Hadi, ever the optimist, jumped in. "What if you text him to stop? Or to leave you alone? He has to listen to you, right? It's in his programming."

"Tried that." Greg sighed. "Didn't work."

"Could you give him an impossible task?" Cyril asked. "Something that would occupy his time forever?"

"Like what?"

"I don't know, I'm just trying to find an easy—"

"There is no easy solution," Greg snapped. "I just . . . need time to think."

As a unit, the boys headed back out the way they'd come in. No one suggested looking around more. Not even Greg. None of them spoke. They just went back outside, got on their bikes, and pedaled hard into fog that was now so thick the restaurant disappeared into it. They pedaled in silence only broken by the pattering rain, the swooshing sound of their wheels on the wet pavement, and their pant-ing breath.

At the corner where they normally stopped to say good-bye before biking on to their respective houses, no one even slowed. They all just headed for home. Greg understood. None of them were ready to talk about what had just happened.

Greg wasn't sorry to get home and find his parents were still out. He was, in fact, relieved they didn't see him. When he looked at himself in the bathroom mirror, he was so pale his features almost disappeared into the blank whiteness of his face.

A long, hot shower brought color back to his skin, and it brought conscious thought back to his mind. Where was Fetch?

Even though he knew Fetch would have had to leave the restaurant to dig up the spider and kill the neighbor's dog, Greg had convinced himself Fetch went back to the restau-rant when his duty was done. The idea of him being out there, somewhere, lurking . . .

The hair on the back of Greg's neck prickled. Suddenly remembering his phone, he stared at the green sweats he'd left crumpled on the floor. His phone was in one of the pockets.

Taking a long breath, he bent over and retrieved the phone, checking for missed texts.

Sure enough. There was Fetch's latest text:

H2CUS.

"Yeah, well, I don't hope to see you soon," Greg muttered.

Greg didn't allow himself to ask all the questions that wanted to be asked after their latest encounter with Fetch. Instead, he decided to concentrate on school for a change, specifically, on Spanish. If he didn't get on top of his Spanish homework, he was going to fail the class. So on Saturday morning, he texted Manuel asking if he had time to help him. Manuel didn't respond.

Greg shrugged. Okay, so he'd have to muddle through on his own. He opened his Spanish workbook and picked up his pencil.

Then he snapped his pencil in half when he realized what he'd just done.

"Oh no!" Greg shouted. He jumped up. He had to get to . . .

"Crap!" He didn't know where he needed to go!

Greg grabbed his phone and called Cyril.

"I'm not going back there," Cyril said.

"That's not why I'm calling. Do you know where Manuel lives?"

"Sure. He's about a half mile up the street from me. That's how we met." He gave Greg an address. "Why do you need . . . ?"

"I've gotta go. Sorry. I'll explain later." Greg shoved his phone in his pocket and tore out of his house. Grabbing his bike, he ignored the steady mist and pedaled as hard as he could.

Greg nearly collapsed in horror when he got to Manuel's house and saw that the front door was wide open. Was he too late?

Right after he'd texted Manuel, he'd realized Fetch could have interpreted that text as instruction to retrieve Manuel. Given what Fetch had done to the neighbor's dog, Greg was afraid Fetch might punish Manuel for not being available to help Greg. Or worse, Fetch might kill Manuel and drag his body to Greg's house. There was no telling what the animatronic beast was capable of.

Dropping his bike on the concrete driveway, Greg ran to the gaping doorway and peered into the tile-covered entryway of the small one-story house. He broke out in a cold sweat when he saw muddy paw prints on the gray squares.

"Manuel?" he shouted, taking a step into the house.

"*¿Que pasa?*" a voice called from behind Greg.

A dog barked.

Greg whirled around. Manuel and a yellow Labrador were standing at the edge of a front yard filled with patches of grass and exposed dirt. The dog had a red ball in its mouth, and its feet were muddy.

Greg's heart, which had been trying to set a speed record, settled into a more normal pace. "Hey, Manuel."

"Hi, Greg." Manuel's smile was friendly but confused.

Not a surprise. How could Greg explain why he was here?

"Um, I sent you a text, but you didn't respond. Needed a bike ride anyway, so I thought I'd stop by—Cyril told me you lived down the street from him. I wondered if you had time to help me with my Spanish."

Manuel's confusion disappeared. "Sure. Sorry about the text. I left my phone inside. I can do it now, if Oro will let us." The dog next to him barked.

Greg, so relieved that he'd imagined danger that didn't exist, grinned at the dog. "Hi, Oro. Want me to throw the ball?"

Oro wagged his tail but didn't move.

Manuel laughed. "He understands Spanish. Say, '*Tráeme la pelota.*'"

Greg repeated the command.

Oro brought him the ball.

Greg laughed. "Maybe I don't need your help. Maybe Oro can help me."

Manual laughed, too, and for the next hour, Greg forgot all about Fetch while he played with Oro and improved his Spanish.

The rest of the weekend passed without any disturbing incidents. And when Monday came, Greg was in a great mood. He was all about his most recent triumph, getting Kimberly as his lab partner. He'd intended it; it had happened. And after his most recent intention with Fetch seemed to thwart him, it looked like Greg was actually learning to use the Zero Point Field. Score!

Greg and Kimberly had their first meet-up after school the next day in the science lab. Every team had been given a set time to use the REG machine Mr. Jacoby got for their experiments. Greg and Kimberly were second to use the machine.

Their assignment was to attempt to control, with their minds, the 0s and 1s generated by the machine. Both were to focus their will on either 0s or 1s (Greg took 0s, and Kimberly took 1s) for a total of ten minutes each. They were to record their results, and then they were supposed to write a paper about some aspect of REG research and how it impacted society. Greg had thought he'd have to be the one to suggest a topic, but Kimberly beat him to it.

Sitting cross-legged on the floor after they used the REG machine, Kimberly said, "I have an idea for the paper." She pulled out her phone and tapped at it. Greg stared at her hands. She had the prettiest hands. Today, her nails were bright blue. They matched the tight blue sweater she wore. He tried not to stare . . .

"Are you listening?"

"I'm sorry. What?"

Even though Greg had known Kimberly for seven years, he was pretty sure he'd never said more than two words to her at a time. Whenever he had the chance to talk to her, his brain drained down his legs and puddled in his shoes. He'd gotten her as a partner now, but how was he going to talk to her?

"I said I think we should write about how REGs influence big world disasters."

Wow. She knew that?

If he hadn't been in love before, he sure was now.

"Yeah," he agreed. "That's perfect."

"You know about it?" She looked up at him.

Greg still sat in his chair, but now he slid down onto the beige-tiled floor so he could see her better. Stoked by her idea, he forgot to be nervous. "Yeah. I've been following the way REGs have been used to study the power of thinking for a couple years."

"That's Gucci!" Kimberly gave him one of her full smiles.

He grinned back like an idiot.

He was so excited about her paper topic that he wasn't as bummed about the fact that Kimberly had done better with the REG machine then he had. No matter how much he concentrated, his machine's results were barely above a normal random readout.

"I tried to talk to my parents about it," Kimberly said. "They're pretty open-minded, but Mom said it was too 'out there,' and Dad said the machines were probably being set up to get the results the people wanted. But they're not!" Kimberly leaned forward, her eyes bright.

Greg couldn't believe she was as into this stuff as he was. "I know," Greg said, leaning in, too.

"And did you know they get spikes before big sporting events?"

He hesitated only a second before saying, "Do you know about Cleve Backster?"

Kimberly blinked. "No. Who's he?"

"He was an interrogation instructor for the CIA, and he taught classes on using the polygraph machine."

"Okay." Kimberly put her elbows on her knees, clearly focused on what he was saying.

He couldn't believe he had her full attention. He tried not to let himself be distracted by her peaches and cream perfume.

"So what about him?" Kimberly prompted.

Greg cleared his throat. "Well, he started using the polygraph machine to do experiments on plants, and he discovered plants can sense our thoughts."

"My mother sings to her plants because she says it makes them grow faster."

Greg nodded. "They probably do."

"That's why I was surprised my mom didn't believe the REG stuff."

"I think it freaks people out," Greg said.

Kimberly nodded. "So is there more about this polygraph guy?"

"Yeah. So Backster experimented with the plant's reactions to his actions. Like, he burned a plant and got a reaction, but not just in the burned plant. Nearby plants reacted, too!

And then he just thought about burning the plants, and the second he had that thought, the polygraph recorded a reaction in all the plants. Like the plants had read his mind."

"Whoa!"

Greg nodded so hard he felt like a bobblehead doll. "Yeah, I know!" He grinned. "Most people didn't believe Backster when he published his results. But he kept experimenting, not only with plants but with human cells, and he proved that cells *can* sense thoughts. They have a consciousness."

Kimberly twirled a lock of her shiny hair with an index finger. "So if cells have consciousness, then why's it such a leap to think our brains can influence a machine?"

"Exactly!"

"We should include that in our paper," Kimberly said. "It's good stuff."

"Yeah. I thought it was so cool that I decided to do my own experiments. My uncle got me a polygraph machine, and I started trying things with my plants. It actually works. They know what I'm thinking . . . well, at least the simple stuff."

"Wow!"

"Yeah. I've been trying other things, too." Greg hesitated. Should he tell her?

"Like what?" she asked.

Greg chewed his lip. Oh, why not? He scooted closer to her and lowered his voice. "Do you remember what Mr. Jacoby said about the Zero Point Field, that it means all matter in the universe is interconnected by subatomic waves that connect one part of the universe to every other part?"

"Yeah, sure."

"Well, I read about the field over the summer, and when I read it, I got really excited. I read that researchers are saying this field could explain lots of stuff no one could explain before, stuff like chi and telepathy and other psychic abilities."

"I have a cousin who's psychic," Kimberly said. "She always knows when there's going to be a test at her school." Kimberly laughed. "I've been trying to get her to teach me how to do that."

Greg grinned. "Then you'll get it."

"Get what?"

"Well, I have some good stuff in my life, but there's so much I hate. Like my dad and . . . well, just stuff. So I figured I could learn to use the field, you know? Communicate with it. Tell it what I want and get it to tell me what to do. So I've been practicing on my plants, seeing if they'd respond to my intention, and then I started just concentrating on things I wanted and seeing if I got any ideas, you know, like . . ."

"Guidance?"

"Yeah."

Kimberly slowly nodded. "I get what you're trying to do." She wrinkled up her perfect nose. "The problem is, well," she shrugged, "I just wonder if trying to get the field to work is like a monkey trying to fly an airplane. He's going to crash and burn before he can figure it out."

Greg tried not to let her see that her words felt like a kick in the gut. She obviously did see, though, "Not that you're a monkey, I mean. I just mean quantum stuff is hard. I like it, too, and I've tried to read about it, but I don't get it. Not really."

"Hey!" Trent White burst into the room. "You two smashing face in here or what?"

Kimberly blushed deep red.

"Shut up, Trent," Greg said.

"Shut up yourself. Your time's up. Our turn." Trent gestured toward his project partner, another school athlete, Rory.

Greg still couldn't believe they were both in Advanced Scientific Theory.

"We're done." Kimberly scrambled to her feet.

She and Greg left the room. "Let's get together over the weekend to talk more about the paper," she suggested.

"Sure."

After Greg got home from school, he texted Hadi and Cyril, asking them to come over.

While he waited, he looked at the latest text from Fetch:

2EZ.

"What's too easy?" Greg responded.

AOTA.

"All of the above what?" Greg asked.

411.

All of the above information was too easy? What did Fetch mean? Was he talking about Greg's conversation with Kimberly? Was he saying that Greg was making the Zero Point Field too easy? And why did Greg care about the opinion of an animatronic dog anyway?

He wanted to ignore Fetch, but then Fetch texted:

REG M2.

Fetch then texted a link to a website that sold small REGs.

Greg didn't understand what Fetch meant by REG M2. Did M2 mean "Me too?" Did that mean Fetch was saying he wanted an REG, too? Or was he saying he was an REG? Or *like* an REG?

Greg frowned and texted back, Thx. He figured whatever Fetch was saying, he should stay on Fetch's good side.

Hadi and Cyril came over and brought pizza. Surprisingly, Greg's parents were home, but they were caught up in some intense discussion and they both said, "Okay," when Greg asked if his friends could come over with pizza.

The boys spent their first fifteen minutes wolfing down pepperoni pizza and guzzling Coke. When Hadi burped, loudly, Greg decided it was time.

"We need to talk about what happened the other night."

"Do we really?" Cyril asked.

"Yeah," Greg said. "Fetch is out there somewhere!"

"Well, now you're just being a moron," Hadi said. "*That's*

what bothers you? That he's out there somewhere? Yeah, he's out there. For sure. Fetch is animatronic, and you obviously managed to turn him on. But how about the fact that Fetch dug up the spider for you or the fact that he *killed a dog* for you?"

"Yeah, there's that," Greg agreed.

"I think we should destroy it," Hadi said.

"I think we should stay away from it," Cyril said.

"Yeah, but will Fetch stay away from us?" Greg asked.

Hadi glared at him. "You're the one who activated it."

Greg threw up his hands. "I didn't even know what I was doing!"

"Well, you need to figure it out," Hadi said. "You're the smart one."

"Yeah," Cyril agreed.

"You sound like you're mad at me," Greg accused his friends.

Cyril looked at his tiny feet. Hadi said, "Well . . ."

"You *are* mad at me! What did I do?"

"You're the one who wanted to go there in the first place," Cyril said.

Greg opened then closed his mouth. He got up. "Fine. You two can head home then. I'll take care of it."

Hadi and Cyril stared at him then looked at each other. "Whatever, dude," Hadi said. "Come on." He got up and gestured for Cyril to follow.

★ ★ ★

An hour later, wearing threadbare sweats and an old tie-dyed T-shirt, lying on his back in bed in the dark, Greg said to the ceiling, "I need money."

If he had money, more money than he could get from babysitting anyway, he could get whatever he needed for his experiments. He could set up his own consciousness project. Then he'd know what to do about Fetch.

Greg grabbed his phone. Over the summer, he'd read an article about this thirteen-year-old entrepreneur who set up a home business and was making tons of profit. Greg was fourteen, and he was smart. Why couldn't he have a business? He thumbed in a search, "how to make money fast."

He spent the next hour skimming through "make money at home" sites. By the end of the hour, he was frustrated, confused, and tired. So he got ready for bed. Just before he laid down, he picked up his phone and sent Dare a text: **I need the Magic Finger of Luck. Can U teach me how to make money?**

Dare didn't respond. Greg figured he was probably asleep. Dare usually went to bed earlier than Greg did.

Before he turned off the light, his phone buzzed. A text from Fetch:

GNSD.

"Sweet dreams to you, too," Greg responded, ignoring the chill that skirted down his spine.

He frowned, bothered by something; but he wasn't sure what it was. He was *so* tired he wasn't thinking straight. He couldn't keep his eyes open. So he closed them, and he was asleep immediately.

When Greg woke up, it was still dark out. He erupted from the bed and blinked frantically to focus. His last text! What had he been thinking?

"Idiot!" Greg grabbed his phone and deleted his text to Dare.

Then he called Dare.

No answer.

He pulled up Dare's landline number and called it. Even if Dare was asleep, that phone would wake him.

No answer.

What should he do?

Greg had no way to get up to Dare's place on his own. It was too far to bike. No buses ran up there. How could he get to Dare and warn him?

A ride. He needed a ride. From who? No way could he ask his parents.

He thought about Mrs. Peters three doors down. She was always nice to him. Maybe . . .

Greg tore off his PJs and pulled on gray sweats and a navy blue hoodie. He grabbed his phone and ran out of his room.

He wasn't sure how he was going to explain to Mrs. Peters why he needed a ride at—what time was it? He checked. Four thirty.

Well, he'd just have to figure it out.

In his stocking feet, Greg took the stairs two at a time. Inside the front door, he stopped to tug on his rain boots in the entryway. Then he threw back the deadbolt and flung the door open. He started to charge through the door.

But then he looked down.

His legs went out from under him, and he crumpled to the ground. He started to heave, covered his mouth, and looked away from what lay on top of the WELCOME FRIENDS mat.

Looking away didn't help, though. The image was indelibly etched into his retinas. In his mind's eye he could see Dare's thick finger, the base torn and bloody, part of the bone jutting through the gore. The finger was dusky and had tufts of light hair. The blood was bright red. Even just in memory, the details were excruciating. Greg even noticed that the blood had congealed before the finger had been dropped on the mat because the white *M* wasn't bloody.

"Greg? What are you doing down here?" Greg's mom was coming down the stairs.

Greg didn't think. He snatched up the finger and stuffed it in the pocket of his hoody. Grabbing the doorframe, he pulled himself to his feet and shut the door.

"I think I was sleepwalking," Greg said. *Lame.* But he was too out of it to come up with something better.

Then he noticed his mom was crying.

"What's wrong?" he asked.

Her eyes and her nose were red. Her mascara was smeared. Her cheeks were wet. She wore nothing but her pink fuzzy robe over a white frilly nightshirt. She wiped her cheeks and sank down onto the third step from the bottom of the stairs.

"What's wrong?" he repeated. He rushed to the stairs and sat next to his mom.

She took his hand. "I'm sorry. It's not the end of the world. I'm just shocked, is all. It's your uncle Darrin."

Greg stiffened.

"You won't believe this!" his mom said, sobbing. "He got attacked by some kind of wild animal. It tore off his finger!"

Greg couldn't breathe. He looked down at his hoody pocket. He put his hand over it, feeling the ring still wrapped around the grotesquely ripped base. When Greg had seen the finger, he'd have known it was Dare's even without the presence of the onyx and gold ring. But the ring? That, more than the exposed bone and veins, was what had dismayed him the most. Now his eyes filled with tears. He cleared his clogged throat and managed, "That's terrible!"

"He's all scratched up, too, mauled. He's been airlifted to the hospital. I just can't believe this."

Greg couldn't comfort her. He was too busy realizing.

"Oh no, no, no," he groaned.

His mother, not understanding, wrapped her arms around him. "It's okay. Really. I'm sure he'll be fine. He'll probably make a joke out of losing his finger." She burst into tears again.

"No, no, no," Greg repeated. It was like a mantra, like he could say it enough and it would make everything stop and go back to the way it was.

Disengaging himself from his mom, he touched the hoodie pocket and said, "I need air." He ran to the front door, threw it open, and careened down the front stairs.

It wasn't raining, but if it had been, he wouldn't have cared. He had to get away. He couldn't face it. He couldn't accept what he'd done.

Because he'd done it. Obviously, *he* had done it.

Greg didn't know where he'd been planning to go when he left his house, but before he could go anywhere, he was stopped in his tracks. Was that . . . ?

Yes, it was.

Under the shore pines clustered near the back of his yard, next to the marram grass at the edge of the dunes, Fetch sat. His eyes glowed red in the now predawn light, and his ears were tilted forward, as if in question. Greg was so angry and upset he didn't even think about running away. Instead, he grabbed the baseball bat from his dad's pile of sporting equipment and took one step toward Fetch. Then another. And another. And then he was sprinting full out.

Fetch stood. Eyes bright, he looked at Greg.

If Fetch had been a real dog, Greg would have thought this was cute. But Fetch wasn't a real dog. He was an animatronic *killer* made to look like a dog. Greg wasn't going to let the seemingly happy look stop him.

When Greg reached Fetch, he didn't hesitate. He swung the bat at Fetch's head.

The first strike split open the top of Fetch's head, revealing a metal skull and ripped wires. Sparks flew as Greg wound up for another swing.

"What did you do?!" Greg screamed at the Fetch.

Fetch's mouth hinged opened in what looked like a silly grin. Greg swung the bat and whacked Fetch's mouth. Metal teeth sprayed out, and more sparks sputtered at the end of wires that hung through the mouth opening.

But Fetch was still looking at Greg with what looked like an eager gaze.

"Stop it!" Greg shrieked.

Swinging the bat in a wide arc, he brought it down on Fetch's head as hard as he could. Metal clanged. More sparks flitted out into the wet dune grass. And Greg kept up his assault. He pounded on Fetch with the bat. Once, twice, three times, four times. Finally, Fetch's face was pulverized. But Greg wasn't done. He raised the bat again and battered what was left of the machine. Soon, the remnants of the animatronic killer didn't resemble anything but a small pile of industrial debris. Still, Greg didn't stop . . . not until he had blisters on his palms, and he was chomping at the sea air in frantic wide-mouthed gulps.

Finally, he dropped the bat.

Greg fell back on his butt in the sloppy wet dunes. He stared at the pile of metal, hinges, synthetic fur, and wires as he sat, catching his breath. The surf was loud, its rhythmic roar like the chant of a million angry men. To Greg, it was the sound of judgment. It was his accuser. How dare he think he knew enough about the field to think about luck and expect to get money? And what was he thinking when he texted Dare about the Magic Finger of Luck? He was the one who'd been wrong. How could he blame this on Fetch?

Fetch might have been like an REG machine in that he seemed to be reacting to Greg's thoughts, but he wasn't an REG machine. Was he?

Greg didn't understand what was going on, but he thought that Fetch was responding to more than just his texts. Somehow Fetch was observing Greg's actions and maybe he was even reading his thoughts the way Greg's plants did. Fetch wasn't the Zero Point Field, but he was part of it. He seemed to be acting like he was the field's dog or something, getting whatever the field thought Greg wanted.

Whatever Fetch was, it was Greg's fault that Dare got his finger torn off.

"Greg, you out there?" Greg's mom called.

Greg looked at the destroyed animatronic.

"Greg?" His mother started down the steps.

Greg and the debris were partially hidden in the marram grass, but if his mom came into the backyard, she'd see them. Greg looked around and spotted a depression under the drift-wood log covered with Fetch's teeth. He quickly shoveled all of Fetch's parts into the hole and called out, "Coming."

His mom wanted Greg to know Dare would be in sur-gery for a while to repair damaged nerves and sew up his lacerations. It would be some time before they could go visit him, so she was going to work until then. She hugged Greg before she left. His dad was already gone. As Greg went inside, he realized he'd left the house without his phone. What if someone had been trying to reach him?

Someone?

Let's get real. He meant Fetch. Had Fetch sent him a text before Greg had spotted him?

Yes. Fetch had texted, Greg discovered when he reached his room. Fetch had asked Greg how he was going to use the Magic Finger of Luck.

This question put Greg into a fetal position on the bed, and it brought on a fresh wave of tears. Kimberly's words played on a repeat track in his head: "He's going to crash and burn before he figures it out."

Crash and burn.

Crash and burn.

Crash and burn.

Greg sat and up and yelled, "Noooo!" He grabbed one of the books from his nightstand, and he fired it at the biggest plant in his collection. The plant went flying off the shelf, and dirt exploded into the air. Greg snatched up another book, threw it. Another book, threw it. He did this over and over until every one of his plants was on the floor, and dirt was everywhere. He breathed in the musky scent of the damp earth.

He laid back down and tried to calm his breathing. This

brought the tears back, but that was okay. He laid there and cried until he fell asleep.

When he woke up, the sun was dropping in the west. It was midafternoon.

As full consciousness returned, he remembered everything.

"What a complete tool," he berated himself.

What had he been thinking? Did he really believe he could figure out what no one else—not the CIA or the universities or the experts had figured out? If it could be done, wouldn't it have *been* done?

Such an egotistical little twerp he'd been. He realized now how little he knew and that meant that whatever he *thought* he knew, whatever he *thought* had been the right thing to do, could have been exactly the opposite of that. Was he really guided to the restaurant? Or did he come up with the lame idea himself? And if he was guided, what guided him? He'd assumed he was doing something to get him what he wanted, but . . .

When his phone rang, he froze.

Then he realized he was being stupid. Fetch didn't call; he texted. Greg looked at his phone. It was Hadi.

"Hey, dude, you okay? You weren't at school."

Greg stared at his destroyed plants. He'd forgotten all about school. He'd forgotten all about life.

"Yeah. Something happened to Dare."

"What? Is he okay?"

"Dude. I'm sorry."

Greg could hear Hadi talking to someone else.

"Cyril says he's sorry, too," Hadi said.

"Thanks."

"Can we do anything?"

"Not unless you can do magic."

"Sorry to disappoint, dude."

"Yeah."

"Hey, I'm not sure it'll make you feel better, but Kimberly was looking for you just now."

Greg sat up and finger-combed his hair, catching himself and rolling his eyes. It wasn't like she was in the room. "Really?"

"Totally. She said you have a good paper idea and she's ready to work on it."

Right. The paper. He slumped. He'd been so excited about that, and now he didn't want to even think about the topic.

Still, if it meant spending time with Kimberly . . .

He noticed Hadi was talking.

"What? Sorry?"

"I said, after listening to you moon over that girl forever, it would be nice to see you with her."

"It hasn't been forever. Just since second grade."

Had it really been that long that he'd loved Kimberly?

"Whatever."

"Yeah, it would be nice to see her."

"Well, then don't miss your chance. Call her and get busy on that paper. Win her over, dude!"

Greg grinned. Then he frowned. It felt wrong to feel hopeful after what had happened to Dare.

"I gotta go," he said.

"Sure. Let us know if you want to hang out."

"Okay."

Greg put down the phone and went to take another hot shower. He stank of sweat and salty sea air.

When he got out of the shower and got dressed, he picked up the phone to call Kimberly. That's when he saw a text from Fetch . . . sent *five minutes ago*. It said:

Will retrieve.

"Noooo," Greg groaned.

Greg shoved his phone in his pocket and tore out of his room. He galloped down the stairs and out to the dunes.

Would Fetch even be there?

When he reached the edge of his yard, he slowed. He was almost afraid to look. But he had to.

He edged into the dunes, and he looked under the driftwood log.

Greg's legs gave out. He sank to his knees in the wet dune grass.

Although a few small screws, metal pieces, wires, and a hinge were strewn out under the log, the vast majority of the scraps were gone. *Gone.*

Greg looked around. The only footprints he saw in the sand were his own. But the sand did tell a story: around the driftwood, the wet sand was grooved with ragged drag marks. At least a dozen smears stretched out from under the log, and then they angled toward each other until they formed one messy drag mark that ended at a flattened clump of dune grass.

Greg struggled to his feet and backed away from the dunes. Turning, he galloped into the house and up to his room. There, he sank to the floor and put his head in his hands.

Snapshots of the last several weeks flashed through his head. The spider. The dead dog—the *torn-up* dead dog. Dare's severed finger.

All Greg had wanted was some luck. He didn't want his uncle's finger. But Fetch obviously took things literally.

Greg had no doubt Fetch was active again. How? Greg didn't know, didn't need to know. He just *did* know that Fetch still worked.

So if Fetch interpreted his request for luck as a need to rip off Dare's finger, how exactly would he "retrieve," and more importantly, what, or *who,* was Fetch going to retrieve? Especially now that Greg had beaten him up?

"No!" Greg jumped up and stuffed his phone in his pocket. Shoving his feet into black running shoes, he flew out of his house.

Kimberly lived about a mile away, farther south on the same street he lived on. It would be a straight shot.

Grabbing his bike, Greg pedaled hard. Of course the

wind was picking up again, and it was coming from the south. His lungs were screaming by the time he'd gotten halfway to her house. He ignored them and pushed on. He had to reach Kimberly before Fetch did.

If it wasn't too late already.

When he reached Kimberly's house, he leaped off his bike and prepared to rush up to the door. But he caught himself when he realized the house was dark. No cars were in the driveway; no one was home.

Kimberly had mentioned her mom usually picked her up after school, and they often stopped to run errands on the way home. If Kimberly was still at school when Hadi called, Greg probably beat them here.

Greg leaned over to catch his breath and picked up his bike. Carrying it to the bushes at the edge of Kimberly's yard, he hunkered down to wait.

He considered searching for Fetch, but he didn't know when Kimberly would get home, and he could miss her if he was off looking for Fetch. He couldn't risk it.

He waited.

While he waited, he tried to calm himself with yoga breathing. It didn't work.

He was so tense by the time the sun started going down at four thirty he felt like his limbs would break if he tried to unbend them from his crouched position. He figured he'd better try to move now before Kimberly got home.

Just as he started to stretch out his legs and stand, he spotted headlights coming up the street. He bent low again.

The car went past, but before he could straighten, another came after it. This was the one.

A dark blue SUV pulled into the driveway. The passenger door opened, and Kimberly, wearing jeans and a cute green top that matched her eyes, bounced out of the car. She was chattering to her mother as she did. "I think if we put the oregano in, it would be good."

"Maybe with basil, too," her mother said.

Tall and slender, with a pretty face and short graying black hair, Mrs. Bergstrom was in her midsixties. When they were in second grade, Kimberly told him her mother was fifty-one years old when Kimberly was born. "I was a miracle baby," Kimberly said. "I figure that means I should be nice to my parents." She laughed her musical laugh.

Greg knew Kimberly's dad was even older than Kimberly's mom. He was retired. He'd owned a couple of the hotels in Ocean Shores, and he'd sold them the year before.

"He mostly plays golf now," Greg overheard Kimberly tell a friend.

Greg had met both of the Bergstroms. Although Mr. Bergstrom was a little grumpy, Mrs. Bergstrom was nice.

But would she listen?

Greg prepared to step out of the bushes and tell Kimberly she was in danger, but he realized how insane his story was going to sound. Maybe if he could talk to just her, she could convince her parents to listen.

Before he decided what to do, a black sedan pulled in behind the SUV. It crunched over gravel strewn across the asphalt driveway, and Mr. Bergstrom got out.

The wind picked up speed just when Mr. Bergstrom's feet hit the ground. It blew off his red baseball cap, and Kimberly skipped after it.

"Thanks, sweetie," Mr. Bergstrom called. He smoothed down thinning white hair and hugged his daughter.

The ocean wasn't as loud now as it had been that morning when Greg was running in the dunes. Was it seriously just that morning that he had found out about Dare and tried to destroy Fetch? It felt like a year ago, at least.

Even though it wasn't as loud, the ocean's insistent murmur drowned out what Kimberly and her parents were saying as they walked toward the house. Greg started to rise again, still not sure what to do.

Just as he rose, Mr. Bergstrom's hat blew off once more, and he strode after it. The hat landed right in front of the bush Greg hid in, and Mr. Bergstrom spotted him.

"Hey, kid, what're you doing in the bushes?" Mr. Bergstrom's voice was strident and sharp.

Greg squared his shoulders and stood up. He had to try to warn them.

"Hi, Mr. Bergstrom," he said.

"Who're you? No, wait. I've seen you."

"Greg, what are you doing here?" Kimberly called out

from her front walk. She came toward Greg and her dad. Mrs. Bergstrom followed.

"Um, Kimberly, I know this is going to sound crazy."

"What's going to sound crazy? What's the meaning of this?" Mr. Bergstrom snapped.

Greg took a deep breath and dove into his explanation. "Kimberly, you're in danger. Like, serious danger. I think, well, I think, someone, er . . . some*thing* is going to try to kill you."

"What?" Mr. and Mrs. Bergstrom erupted in unison. Mr. Bergstrom's tone was rough and outraged. Mrs. Bergstrom's tone was a high-pitch shriek of fear.

Kimberly said nothing, but her eyes had widened.

"Kimberly, you know what we were talking about, the REGs, the plants, the cells, the shared consciousness, the guidance?"

She nodded.

"I have no idea how to explain this, but part of the guidance I got was that I had to know what was inside that abandoned pizzeria. So I got Cyril and Hadi to break in there with me . . ."

"You what?" Mr. Bergstrom sputtered.

Greg ignored him. "And we found this animatronic dog that's designed to sync up with your cell phone."

Mr. Bergstrom tried to interrupt again, but Greg talked louder and faster. "I was curious, so I poked around at it, and I couldn't get it to work. Or at least I thought I couldn't get it to work. But apparently I did, because it's been texting me and doing things for me. At first it did helpful things, but then it started doing things I didn't want it to do. It killed a dog that bothered me . . ."

Kimberly, a dog lover, Greg knew, sucked in her breath.

He shrugged at her. "Yeah, I know. It was awful. I mean, this was a horrible dog, but still, it was a dog, and the way it was killed was . . . Anyway, then I was wanting some luck, and my uncle had this Magic Finger of Luck, and I wished I had that, too, and then I found his . . ."

"Young man," Mr. Bergstrom shouted.

Greg ignored him and talked even louder. "I found his finger. And so this afternoon, I said, well, I said I wanted to be with you, and now I'm afraid Fetch is going to—"

"Young man!" Mr. Bergstrom yelled.

Greg stopped because, well, what else could he say?

That's when he noticed Mr. Bergstrom put a cell phone to his ear, "Yes, could you please send an officer to my home? Some crazy teenager is stalking my daughter. I want him arrested."

Greg looked at Kimberly. She mouthed, "Sorry."

He shook his head.

He'd failed again.

When the police officer questioned Greg about breaking into the restaurant, Greg kept telling himself Kimberly would be okay. She was fine now, and if Fetch was following what was going on through Greg's cell phone, he'd surely know Greg wanted Kimberly to be left alone.

"I'd forgotten all about that old pizzeria," the middle-aged cop said when Mr. Bergstrom reported Greg's break-in. "Is it still there?"

Is it still there? Greg thought. Was the place like Brigadoon or something?

When the police officer put Greg in his SUV and took him to the police station, Greg kept telling himself Kimberly would be okay. Her parents would be on guard. Fetch wouldn't be able to "retrieve" her.

But no matter how often he told himself everything would be fine, he dreaded going back to his house. It took two hours for the police to process him and question him. It took another two hours for the police to locate his parents and another hour and a half for them to get to the station because they were both in Olympia. What if Fetch had gotten to Kimberly in that time?

His parents finally showed up at the station, his mother red-eyed and his dad pissed off about, well, everything. The police had decided to release Greg into his parents' care. He'd be free, which also meant he could keep an eye on Kimberly. As soon as his parents went to bed, he'd sneak out and go watch over her. He'd do that for as long as it took him to find Fetch and figure out a way to deactivate him.

Greg almost couldn't bear to get out of his dad's pickup when his dad pulled it into the garage. Dragging his feet,

Greg reluctantly opened the car door and stepped onto the concrete. He cautiously approached the stairway leading up to the front door. Then he steeled himself and looked around.

Everything seemed normal. Kimberly's body wasn't under the house or on the front mat.

He nearly fainted in relief.

"What the hell's wrong with you?" Greg's dad asked when Greg sagged against the stair railing.

"Nothing."

When Greg and his parents entered their house, Greg's dad grabbed Greg's arm. Greg gritted his teeth.

"I'd say I was disappointed in you," his dad said, "but I haven't expected anything good from you in years."

Greg's mom sighed. "Steven."

"Hillary."

Greg ignored them both and went up the stairs to his room.

Peeling off his clothes as soon as he was in the darkened space, he went to take yet another shower. He stank . . . again. Not only did the hard bike ride and the panic to save Kimberly make him sweat buckets, he'd sat in what smelled like dried urine in the cop's SUV.

He thought the hot shower might bring him back to life. He had to get the energy to go to Kimberly's house again. His bike was still in the back of his dad's pickup. The police-man had stuck it in his SUV when he took Greg in, and he'd given it back when he and his parents left the station.

But when Greg got out of the shower, he was wiped out.

He looked at the time on his phone. He also checked for texts. Nothing. That was good. Right?

Maybe he could take a nap before heading to Kimberly's to be sure she was okay. Heck, maybe he'd been wrong about the whole thing. Maybe Fetch was retrieving him a snack or information he hadn't even realized he'd requested. Maybe there really was nothing to worry about.

Greg pulled on a yellow T-shirt and a pair of gray flannel sleep pants. Then he threw open the bathroom door.

Barely containing a scream, Greg stumbled away from the door and fell to the tiled floor, his mind struggling to accept what he was looking at.

There was something wrapped in a sheet, laying across the doorway. As he stared, the once beige sheet was turning a deep, dark red, and it glistened wet in the room's muted light.

Who was under the sheet? What was under the sheet? Greg couldn't get himself to move so he could find out.

Greg didn't need to look any further. He knew everything he needed to know.

The phone on Greg's bathroom counter vibrated. He couldn't help himself; he picked it up and looked at it.

Fetch had texted:

CU.

LONELY
FREDDY

Bad," Alec had always argued, was such a subjective word. With its very definition, it was determined by someone else's baseline. It was a word that served one purpose: to judge. And Alec had been judged his entire life.

His first memory was a decidedly terrible one. He was in preschool and bigger than the other kids. Recognizing this advantage at an early age, he found he could move to the front of any line with surprising ease. The other kids were glad to play the games he dictated, and he never had to look for a seat at the lunch table. It was only when his preschool teacher pulled him to the side on that first memorable day that Alec was made to understand that he was "bad."

"You're a bully," the teacher had said to him, a word he assumed was positive and smiled when she offered it. Instead of patting him on the shoulder like his mom would do when he ate his whole meal, the teacher shrank away from him in horror. In fact, it was that precise expression on his preschool teacher's face that Alec remembered most of all. More than the way the blue plastic chairs in the classroom would stick to the backs of his legs in summertime. More than the way a fresh box of unused crayons smelled under his nose. More than the way the canned peaches they served as snacks slid around on his tongue amid the sticky syrup and metallic aftertaste.

Alec didn't even remember his preschool teacher's name. He simply remembered her look of horror when he didn't understand that he was "bad."

As he grew older, Alec came to realize that "bad" was defined by comparison. And that was mostly a workable construct for Alec.

Until Hazel came along.

Hazel, who was named after a beloved grandmother Alec had never met. Hazel, whose fine blonde ringlets were twisted up in stiff bows. Hazel, who slept through the entire night with nary a fuss.

Alec was named after no one. It was a compromise between the "Alexander" his mom had wanted and the "Eric" his dad had lobbied for. Alec's curls were unruly, tamed with water from the tap and a wooden-backed brush. Alec's nights were cleaved by nightmares and bouts of loud wakefulness.

For the first five years of his life, Alec's behavior was more or less in constant search of the walls separating good from bad. After Hazel was born, Alec jumped the wall and landed in uncharted lands. He was not as easily tracked in this new space. He was "bad" sometimes, yes, but more often than not, he was boundless. He went undiscovered. It was in that space that "good" and "bad" didn't exist. If there was no one guiding him to the boundaries—if there was no one watching—behavior, if anything, was an afterthought.

"Maybe don't single him out as often, Meg," Alec's aunt Gigi would say. "Kids respond so much better to positive reinforcement."

Aunt Gigi had also suggested to Alec's mom in that same conversation that she switch to organic milk; the added hormones in regular dairy increased aggression in kids, according to some studies. Aunt Gigi had no children and no desire for any. Alec's mom was often in the mood for advice, and her older sister was always happy to give it.

"Gigi, it's not the milk," Alec's mom had argued. "They drink the same milk. And he's not aggressive. He's just . . . I don't know . . . he's in his own world. It's like the rules don't apply to him."

"Well, then you know he'll be a leader when he's older. That's great!" Aunt Gigi had posited.

"Yeah," Alec's mom had said. "Maybe. I don't know. He doesn't seem to like other people much."

"He's ten, Meg. They hate everyone."

"Not everyone," his mom had argued. "Look at Gavin."

"Who?"

"Becca's son."

"That kid who's always smiling at everyone?"

"That isn't a bad thing," his mom had said.

"No, it's a creepy thing," Aunt Gigi had said. "Trust me, you don't want more little Gavins running around the world. That's the kind of kid you find standing over your bed one night holding a butcher knife. No, thanks."

It was times like those that Alec wondered if he'd been born to the wrong sister, and Aunt Gigi was really his mom. But his turned-up nose and blond hair like hay were dead ringers for his mom, no question.

It was also times like these that Alec wished he wasn't so good at eavesdropping. His parents had both warned him about it many times, but inevitably, he'd find himself perched at the top of the staircase, listening to the conversations no one really tried that hard to hide. It was almost like they wanted him to hear.

Eavesdropping was how he'd found out about The Plan.

Alec probably should have seen it coming; it was April after all. The magical miracle month, otherwise known as the month their precious Hazel was born. Alec got a day, the eighteenth day of August to be precise. That was his special day when his parents pretended he wasn't a problem. But Hazel? Hazel got a full thirty days of adoration.

"Someone's got a special day coming up in two weeks," his dad would say.

"Are you excited for your party?" his mom would ask.

And Hazel's eyes would glitter, and she'd act like it was all too much fuss, and his parents would eat it up. She'd earned it, they would say. She should enjoy it. Then they'd look at Alec and wait for him to agree, which he rarely did. Why bother? It's not like it would change a thing; she'd still get the party. Maybe it would have been decent of him to be nice to Hazel once in a while, but Alec just couldn't see giving his parents the satisfaction.

So when he overheard his parents discussing The Plan, he was frankly surprised it had taken them this long to come up with it. They must have been behind on their reading.

"It's in Chapter Five. Have you gotten to Chapter Five yet?" Alec's mom asked his dad across the kitchen table where they stirred their decaf coffee that night.

"I thought Chapter Five talked about letting the child choose his own road," his dad said. That tone of exasperation in his voice was becoming more of a regular thing.

"No no no, that's from *The Glowing Child*," corrected his mom. "I'm talking about *The Plan Planner*. This doctor says *The Glowing Child*'s theories are all wrong!"

Alec remembered *The Glowing Child* method well. Apparently, that author believed every child was simply a blob of clay waiting to be self-molded, which involved some completely bonkers exercises like letting Alec rename himself. So he decided on Captain Thunder Pants and spent the entire week farting himself around the house and claiming he couldn't help it—it was his namesake.

That wasn't as ridiculous as the time they read that they needed to plant a garden with him so he could nurture something, or the time they were told to go camping as a family to get back to their "familial core." The garden experiment ended when Alec buried his mom's wedding ring in the soil to see if it would grow more diamonds. The camping trip devolved into a sort of *Lord of the Flies* situation after Hazel got a mosquito stuck up her nose, and Alec may or may not have convinced her that it would lay eggs in her nasal passage. The trip really didn't have a chance after that.

"Honestly, Meg, the more we read, the more I'm convinced that none of these so-called doctors know what the heck they're talking about," his dad said, but Alec's mom was not one to be deterred.

"Well, Ian, what's the alternative? Do we give up?"

This wasn't the first time Alec had heard a conversation like this one. It seemed to happen in the spaces between every other book that his parents would read to try to understand why their son was just so different than them.

It wasn't the first time Alec had heard this sort of conversation, and yet, it would form the same hard stone in his stomach every single time. Because no matter how many books they read or gardens they made him plant or organic milk they poured down his throat, the one thing they never tried was talking to him.

"Of course we don't give up," his dad said to his mom, whipping his little teaspoon around the sides of his coffee mug until Alec imagined it forming a little decaf whirlpool against the ceramic.

"Just ask me," Alec whispered, and for just a second—for once in all of his fifteen years—his parents were both silent, and he thought maybe they'd hear him. "Just ask me what's the matter."

If they'd asked, he might have said, "I'm not like you, and I'm not like Hazel, and that should be okay."

But his parents simply went on talking.

"You just need to skip ahead to Chapter Five," his mom said.

"Can't we just skip ahead to the part where you tell me what we're supposed to be doing?" his dad said.

"Just read the chapter, Ian. The party's next weekend, and I really think we need to lay some groundwork before Saturday."

His dad sighed so heavily, Alec could hear it from the stairs, which is how he knew that his dad would once again read a useless book about some useless method for helping them to understand their enigma of a child.

It was the same every time.

And because his parents always stashed their collection of parenting books in some supersecret location Alec had never been able to discover, he'd be starting from a disadvantage like always, watching The Plan and Chapter Five's contents unfold over the course of the next week.

Upstairs, in the Jack-and-Jill bathroom that separated Alec's room from Hazel's, he stared in the mirror and tried to see himself the way his parents did. They saw the same blond hair, the same light green eyes, the same jaw set in rigid determination to never hang open in amazement, to never break into an unexpected smile. Alec was nothing if not deliberate.

It was only Hazel who occasionally took him by surprise.

"Are you okay?" she asked from her doorway, and he fixed his face in annoyance, but he was a little too late in doing so, and he was afraid she'd seen him startled.

"Why wouldn't I be?" he asked, leveling her with the same type of question he always asked. He had mastered the art of deflection.

Hazel shrugged and grabbed her toothbrush, playing at being nonchalant, too, but she wasn't nearly as good at it as he was.

"Mom and Dad are acting weird again," she said, short-hand for the explanation. She meant "Mom and Dad are picking on you again." But Alec wasn't so easily fooled. His sister was the worst of them. She conned everyone else with her questions that pretended to be innocent, and her smile that might've made anyone else think she meant it.

"Don't worry," he said. "It won't affect your party."

He'd meant for it to be a slight on her, but she misunderstood and thought he actually cared.

"I don't really care that much about the party, you know," she said, looking at his reflection in the mirror instead of looking directly at him. That's how he knew she was lying.

She started to brush her teeth, and Alec took a moment to study her as she looked down into the sink to spit.

It's almost like she was able to will every part of herself to be perfect. Her hair never frizzed. Her nose never ran. Her freckles were evenly spaced, as though they'd been painted on by a steady hand. Even her teeth were straight. She'd probably never need braces. Alec had started to believe he'd never get his braces *off*.

"Don't be dumb," he finally said. "Of course you care about your stupid party."

Her face flushed a perfectly even shade of pink. "I bet not that many people will even come," she said.

Alec couldn't even muster a response to such a ridiculous plea for fake sympathy. He just snorted.

"Yeah, okay," he said and left her to finish swishing the toothpaste from her mouth. The day of getting his own bathroom in his own house with his own rules and no one to wonder why he was so different than them . . . that day couldn't come soon enough.

Stars had begun to dot the sky when Alec's trance was broken by the creak of the bathroom door on Hazel's side. He waited for the interruption to pass, but the longer he waited, the more it became clear that Hazel wasn't in there to go to the bathroom. After another few seconds, the door to his room from the bathroom opened a crack, and in spilled the blonde curls of his sister as she broke a cardinal rule.

"Get out," he said, and she snatched her head back into the bathroom, startled. But that didn't last.

Instead, she opened the door a little wider, and to Alec's utter disbelief, she dared to take a step inside his room.

He watched her look around for a second, as though she'd entered a strange new world, and in a way, she had. If he'd ever suspected that she snuck in here when he wasn't around, that question was answered by the way she stared around her now. She was a rule follower, even when no one was looking.

"You have a death wish," he said, and he could hear her swallow.

Still, she took another step toward him.

He had a couple of options. The usual verbal intimidation wasn't working. He could use brute force. Pain was an excellent motivator. He could play at charging her: whip the covers off of himself and lunge out of the bed just far enough to chase her off.

Or he could exercise psychological trickery. He could lie there, perfectly still, saying not even a single word more. He could watch her as closely as he was watching her now, wait for her to get close, to achieve whatever insane goal she must have for coming in here and defying all logic, and watch her courage falter the deeper she ventured into his room.

Maybe it was the thrill of exerting that level of control over the situation, or maybe he was curious to see what she'd do. Either way, he opted for the third option.

And he waited.

Strangely, for as closely as he studied her, Hazel studied him just as closely back. She took another step toward his bed, then another, and though he could tell she was trembling, could see that from the second she popped her head in, she continued to walk forward. It wasn't until she was just a couple of steps from his bed that he noticed she was holding something.

She took the last two steps fast, as though her courage was expiring, and set the thing at the foot of Alec's bed. Then she took two steps backward, spinning on her heel, and sprinted back into the bathroom, pulling the door to his bedroom closed behind her.

Alec stared at the book at the foot of his bed for a long time before he finally picked it up.

It was green with bold white lettering, the title precisely centered and slightly raised from the jacket. It was flagged with a bright pink sticky note right at the start of Chapter Five. And when he opened it, written in the fine pencil script of his mother's careful hand, were notes for his dad and her to follow in the days leading up to Golden Hazel's party.

Defying their parents—defying all logic and rules and self-interest—Hazel had stolen *The Plan Planner* from their parents' secret library while they slept.

And she had shared it with him.

Alec's heart raced as he read through the carefully prescribed steps of Chapter Five, the method that promised to turn their bad child good and achieve the familial harmony his parents had read over and over was achievable.

Then, when he was done thumbing through the pages his father hadn't yet bothered to read but had agreed to try out on their problematic first-born, Alec stared at the closed bathroom door his sister had gathered the courage to open, knowing the wrath she'd surely incur. He wondered for the rest of the night about why she had done it. What sort of game was she playing at? What kind of sorcery was she practicing, trying to lull him into a false sense of camaraderie?

Then he allowed his memory to fall backward. He retraced the times he had confused her in the past, the moments he'd simply assumed she was attempting to throw him off of his game. There was the time she baked him cookies in her toy oven after his parents had ignored his pleas for sweets at the grocery store. There was that one moment during the doomed camping trip when she'd laughed at an unintentional joke he'd made, even as she clawed desperately at her nose for the rogue mosquito. There was that one Mother's Day when she'd added his name to the card because he'd forgotten.

Alec stared out his window for the rest of the night, until the dotted stars gave way to the blue dawn before sunrise. It was too tempting to believe that his sister had brought him the book because an alliance had suddenly seemed like a good idea. Ten years of watching the uncanny spells she could cast on his parents and the rest of the world had taught him she wasn't to be so easily trusted.

No, he thought as night crept into day. *This is just another trick.*

She'd been able to fool everyone else but him up to this point. A phony peace offering wasn't about to trick him into thinking she was suddenly on his side. Still, it unsettled him a little that he didn't know what exactly she was up to. There was really only one way to solve that mystery.

"I'll play along," he whispered to himself. "She'll show her cards eventually."

"You're making it too complicated," Hazel said. It seemed she was taking to this new alliance with surprising comfort.

They were sitting by the pool in the backyard, their feet dangling in the chlorinated water as the sun beat against their backs. Alec didn't need a mirror to know his neck was starting to glow pink.

"What're you talking about? It's the perfect plan," he said.

Alec was in such a habit of coldly dismissing his sister, it was exceptionally difficult to pretend to take her seriously.

But if he was going to discover whatever trap it was she was trying to lure him into, he had to be convincing.

Strangely, though, in pretending to take her advice, he was starting to see her differently. It was weird the way this person he was so closely related to was suddenly becoming whole in front of him, like he'd been living with a hologram this whole time.

She was a completely formed con artist.

"So let me get this straight," she said, rolling her eyes skyward. "Your big plan to get Mom and Dad to stop thinking you're a total sociopath is to act like a total sociopath?"

After reading Chapter Five the night before, Alec learned that The Plan was a grossly simplistic take on the teenaged brain. If parents wanted a well-behaved, predictable child, they simply needed to treat them as the opposite of that. It was the worst in hokey reverse psychology, and nothing irked Alec more than having his intelligence insulted.

So his Counterplan was simple; he'd just act worse—way, way worse. He was pretending, of course. He knew his Counterplan was a terrible one. But he needed Hazel to be the one to come up with the idea, not him. It was the only way to make her believe he was falling for her gesture of sibling love.

Once her guard was down, he'd be able to figure out what she was *actually* up to.

"How am I the sociopath in this scenario?" he asked,

trying hard not to actually feel offended. *It's just an act*, he reminded himself. *It's just an act.* "They think the best way to make me good is to treat me like I'm bad!" Alec added in mock outrage. "If you ask me, that's pretty sociopathic."

Now he was *fake*-arguing that *fake* acting bad was the best way to counteract his parents' *fake*-anger at his *real* bad behavior. It was all getting very meta. Alec could feel a headache forming behind his eyes.

"Look," said Hazel, suddenly sounding older than her almost ten years. "Don't take this the wrong way, but you've sort of been losing your touch."

"My touch?" Alec said, putting his hand on the hottest part of his neck to try and shield it. Only yesterday, Hazel would have been terrified to be this blunt with him. Maybe he really was losing his knack for intimidation.

"You used to be pretty good at hiding it," she said, and she looked hard at him, so he knew she was waiting for him to catch on.

When he didn't answer, she sighed and said, "You used to get away with a lot more."

"How's that my fault?" he said, not really liking the way he sounded pouty. "If anything, it's *your* fault!"

She blinked at him slowly.

"They only started to think I was the *bad* one when they figured out you were the *good* one."

Hazel looked back down at the water, and this time, he thought maybe he saw something of the old Hazel, the one who seemed to tiptoe around him with an apology on her lips, like it was a lost cause thinking they'd ever be friends.

To Alec's great amazement, he felt a twinge of remorse for that, a feeling he quickly buried.

"Okay, what's *your* Counterplan?" he asked.

Her solution was too simple.

"Be good," she said.

Alec laughed. What else could he do?

"That's your master class in playing our parents? Reverse-reverse psychology?"

She shrugged. "If you're a little bit better, and I'm a little bit worse, maybe it'll neutralize the attention enough for them to leave us alone for a change."

Alec let his jaw do that thing where it dropped. He let his body experience the full shock he had restrained for so long, and he did it in front of the least likely person: Golden Hazel. The child who did what she was told when she was told to do it. The straight As and the coordinated piano fingers, the dish clearer and the classroom helper. The easy parent/teacher conference. The perfect child.

Maybe she didn't want to be perfect anymore.

How had it never occurred to him that his lot in the family was just as burdensome as hers? Why had the tiny sparkle in her eye never caught his attention, the one that said, "Let's trade places for today"? When had she stopped being Golden Hazel and simply started being Hazel: a kid?

All the more reason not to trust her, he thought, his resolve hardening. She was tired of pretending to be the good one. She was ready to advance to full bad-kid status. Which meant she was definitely up to something.

"Do you think you can do it?" he asked, not meaning it as a challenge but as an actual question. "Be bad?"

"Can *you* be *good*?" she asked, and from her, it definitely *was* a challenge.

They agreed to test her theory that night as a sort of trial run. Their parents were obviously committed to their own experiment prescribed by *The Plan Planner.* They'd been on Alec's case all day: They'd scolded him for failing to pull his clothes from the clothesline. They'd admonished him for playing video games before completing his homework, even though it was spring break. They'd even lectured him on the importance of flossing, a strange battle to pick after a spotless checkup during his most recent dental cleaning.

By the time dinner rolled around, Alec's face hurt from smiling. His neck was sore from nodding. His blood had boiled so many times that day, he was surprised he hadn't cooked from the inside out. He'd swallowed every scolding, never caving to the temptation of sassing his parents.

And true to her word, at each confrontation throughout the day, Hazel had been there to take a portion of the burden away from Alec. She'd chosen that morning to show their mom the less-than-stellar grade on her spelling test from the previous week. She'd "accidentally" dropped her dad's shirts in the mud when she pulled them from the clothesline. And in response to the Great Flossing Debate of Monday afternoon, she'd marked a first for herself: Hazel mouthed off.

"How many cavities did you have at your last checkup?" she muttered within earshot of their mother.

"Young lady, what's gotten into you today?" their mom said.

And as Alec and Hazel rounded the corner to retreat to their separate bedrooms after dinner time, they'd tapped fingertips and hid their smiles.

But as soon as Alec closed his own bedroom door, he reviewed every moment from the day to analyze his sister's actions: the way she'd jump in too readily to deflect the scolding meant for him, the way she'd been so ready with a smart comeback to their mom, the time she winked conspiratorially at him at the dinner table. It was all just a little too perfect, this little show she was putting on for him.

You're not clever enough to play this game, he thought that night before he went to bed. *You're in way over your head, Sis.*

He had five years on her of playing the role of the bad seed. If she thought she was going to usurp that title, she was in for a rude awakening.

The next day was more or less a repeat of the previous one.

When their parents decried Alec's lack of manners at the breakfast table, Hazel burped. When Alec's dad accused him of scratching the side of the car with his bike, Hazel unapologetically took the blame. When Alec's mom wondered aloud when the last time was that Alec had ingested a vegetable, Hazel's quick response was to ask when the last time was that their parents had cooked an edible one.

That night, as Hazel joined Alec on his perch at the top of the stairs, they listened to their parents puzzle through the past two days.

"Is it just me, or does Hazel seem to be going through a . . . phase?" their mom whispered to their dad, teaspoons clinking against the sides of their coffee mugs.

"I thought it was just my imagination at first," their dad agreed.

Their parents' awe was unmistakable.

"Did you hear what she said to me this afternoon?" their mom asked. "She actually said she thought I was starting to look 'haggard'! Haggard, Ian! Do I look haggard?"

"No, but you *sound* haggard," Alec muttered.

Hazel had to stifle her laugh, but Alec was too irritated to find the humor. His parents were infuriating. Was it really so unbelievable that Hazel could be even nastier than predictably rotten Alec?

"Well, could anyone blame you for being haggard?" their father said.

"Oooh, wrong answer," Hazel whispered, and this time, Alec did find the humor, and his laugh caught him off guard.

"So then I *do* look haggard?" their mom said, and Alec could hear a teaspoon clinking faster and faster against the ceramic. One of them was compulsively stirring.

"Of course not, Meg. Can we try to focus on the kids?" he said, and their mom let out a single, uncharitable "Ha!"

"Oh, now look who's ready to be the adult," said their mom, and Alec and Hazel both leaned back on their step, grimacing.

"That's not going to go over well," said Alec.

"Really, Meg?"

"I just think that—"

"Oh, I know what you think. You've made that pretty clear."

"Good grief, Ian, grow up."

But when Alec looked over at Hazel, she was simply smiling. As though the whole thing were going exactly according to plan. Of course, from her perspective, it was.

Then she turned her smile to him. If Alec hadn't been able to see right through her, he might have been tempted to believe it was genuine. If he were the type to fall for such an obvious manipulation, he might have even felt a hint of warmth toward her, a sister simply in search of an actual relationship with her brother.

It was kind of cute, he thought, how she believed she could outsmart him.

"Okay, okay," their dad said, and Alec heard him pull in a deep breath. "We can't turn on each other."

Their mother sighed. "You're right. Let's just go to bed. It's been a long day. Oh, and I can't find the book, FYI."

"Forget it," their dad said. "We'll look for it in the morning."

Two sets of chair legs scraped against the kitchen tiles, and Alec and Hazel jumped to their feet and slipped into their rooms just as the light on the stairs switched on, announcing their parents' approach.

Lying in bed, Alec thought through all the variations in his own plan, the Counter to the Counterplan, as it were.

Tomorrow was party-planning day. He'd heard his mom remind his dad about it a thousand times, not that it mattered since he'd be at work and she would be dragging Alec and Hazel along to meet Aunt Gigi at the pizzeria instead.

It was there that Alec would really ramp up his reconnaissance. If he was going to discover what Hazel was actually up to, he would discover it in the place where all of these plans and counterplans were to culminate. He could think of no other reason for why Hazel was so determined to sabotage her own birthday party by allowing Alec to be . . . well, himself. It had something to do with her birthday on Saturday. Whatever she was planning, it would all go down then.

Alec's only real option was to sit back and let Hazel show her cards. It was a matter of time before it happened, and though she'd proven herself more cunning than he'd originally given her credit for, she was no evil genius.

That title was reserved for Alec.

Sometime after Alec heard his parents' bedroom door shut for the night, the door from the bathroom he shared with Hazel opened, and she poked her head inside.

"Today was fun," she said, and Alec made a quick switch to his "conspiring brother" act.

"Yeah," he said. "Nice job with the cooking dig," he said. "Thanks."

Hazel laughed shyly.

Oh please, Alec thought, but he managed to keep from rolling his eyes.

"Hey, you don't think we're gonna, like, break them or anything, do you?" Hazel said.

"Nah," he said. "They can handle it. Trust me, I've put them through a lot worse."

Hazel nodded, then gave him one more shy smile before shutting the door and padding across the bathroom back to her own room.

It was a few minutes before Alec noticed that he was smiling, too. Not smiling because he was recounting all the ways he'd beaten his sister at her own game. Not smiling because he'd exposed her for the fraud she is for their parents and friends and everyone else in the world to see. Not yet, anyway.

He was smiling because he was enjoying her company.

Get a grip, Alec, he scolded himself.

Then he repeated to himself over and over that she wasn't

as good as she pretended to be, that she was only using him as a means to an end. He reminded himself that this alliance was false and temporary, that once he'd revealed her as a fraud, they'd go back to their separate ends of the bathroom, and Alec could proceed unfettered in doing whatever it was he wanted to do, only this time without the constant comparison to Golden Hazel.

Then he wiped that pathetic smile from his face and fell asleep with vengeance on his mind.

"Gigi, what do you think? Should we kick in for the extra Fazbear Funwiches?"

Alec and Hazel's mom was a wreck on Wednesday. She'd overslept her alarm and had to shove Alec and Hazel into the car without taking a shower or even brushing her teeth. Her hair was jammed into submission under an old baseball cap, and the dark circles under her eyes made her look almost skeletal under the shadow of the hat brim.

Hazel hadn't made it much better by asking her—in her most concerned voice—if she was coming down with something because she looked absolutely sickly. And Alec hadn't made it any better by being . . . nice.

"You look fine, Mom," he'd said, which threw their mom for such a loop, she could only blink at them both before snapping at them to buckle up and running two stop signs in order to meet Aunt Gigi on time at Freddy Fazbear's.

Now she was standing in the party room with a

thoroughly unenthused Party Prepper who was waiting impatiently on answers about Saturday.

"What on earth is a Funwich?" Aunt Gigi asked, leaning her hand on a table and immediately lifting it after detecting something sticky.

"It's a . . . um . . . it's a . . . ." their mom tried, but she was distracted by the sight of Alec and Hazel seeming to play together by the Skee-Ball machines.

"You are truly terrible at this game," Alec said.

"I am not!" said Hazel, but after her third gutter ball in a row, Alec just laughed.

"Okay, it's not my best event," she said. "I shine more in the Pinball category."

"Can you even see over the controllers?" he asked, rubbing the top of her head roughly.

Hazel smiled, and so did Alec, but for a different reason. He felt refreshed after a good night's sleep, renewed in his mission to bring his sister down.

"It's a delicious crescent roll stuffed with your choice of fried macaroni, tater tots, or chocolate marshmallow," the Party Prepper deadpanned to Aunt Gigi.

"That sounds utterly repulsive," Aunt Gigi said.

The Party Prepper didn't argue.

"Yeah, but it's only twenty dollars more, and honestly, I'm just not sure if the Super Surprise Party Package comes with enough food," their mom fretted, finally taking her gaze from the kids and returning to the task at hand.

"So that's a yes on the Fazbear Funwich platter with extra dipping sauces?" said the Party Prepper, by now having had just about enough of this entire interaction.

"Yes. Let's do it," said their mom, clearly relieved at having made the big decision. "I have these coupons from the paper for Foxy's Pirate Palooza special? Can I use those?"

While their mom and Aunt Gigi ironed out the last of the details, Alec and Hazel wandered the empty pizzeria out of earshot of their mom and aunt.

"So what's the big deal with this place anyway?" Alec said, worried he was giving himself away.

The deep, dark truth was that he'd always wanted his own birthday party at Freddy Fazbear's, but he'd never made enough friends to justify the expense of a big party. Instead, his parents had always thrown together a haphazard celebration at home and called it a "pool party," but it was hard to ignore the reality that the only other kids there were all Hazel's friends she'd been allowed to invite in order to fill out the crowd.

Hazel shrugged, feigning nonchalance. "I dunno."

"Liar," he said. "You've had your birthday here for the last four years in a row."

It was the perfect double-psych-out. He'd goad her into telling him what was so important about her stupid party this year, and she'd just think he was trying to have a brotherly conversation with her.

"Why don't you tell me?" she challenged, catching Alec

midstare. He hadn't realized what he was looking at until Hazel did, then he quickly looked away.

"Nice try," she said, tilting her head toward the Yarg Foxy onstage.

There he was in all his Pirate-y, foxy greatness—this eye-patched, peg-legged, hook-wielding orange fox. In this restaurant, he was positioned as a human-size plush figure propped by the stage, presumably there for taking pictures with. But he played a different role in every Freddy Fazbear's, sometimes greeting visitors at the door, sometimes playing in the band onstage with the others. Wherever he was, though, Alec saw him. He was without a doubt Alec's favorite character. It's possible—*possible*—that he used to stick his foot in a plastic flower pot and roll a cardboard tube around his hand and pretend to be Yarg Foxy.

Clearly, it was also possible that Hazel had at some point silently witnessed said roleplay.

"Whatever," he said. "Stupid kid stuff. And besides, we're talking about you, not me."

They were standing in the aisle between the arcade and the stage now. Alec eyed the platform where Freddy Fazbear and all his friends performed animatronic routines. He was always a little unsettled by the way their robotic bodies were eerily still after the show, while the rest of the restaurant chimed with the clinks and buzzers of the games.

He backed away from the stage unconsciously, and was only aware that he'd moved when the back of his heel hit something. He turned to find himself uncomfortably close to a raised platform holding a smaller version of the bear onstage, only this bear had an unlit sign over it that read LONELY FREDDY.

It was a weird name for a toy, but the weirdest parts of it were harder to define. The bear stood stiff, almost at attention. Its eyes stared straight ahead at the stage, but Alec had the strangest feeling that it was still watching him.

"Maybe I want this year to be different," Hazel said, and Alec jumped a little at her voice. He'd gotten so lost in the staring Freddy that he forgot she was standing right there.

"So what, you want more presents?" he asked. "You know you're going to get everything you want anyway," he said, and this time, he let a little of the venom escape. He couldn't help it. How ungrateful could she be? He was the one who nobody liked, who had to fight for everything, who was constantly misunderstood.

"There's some stuff even Mom and Dad can't do," she said, and if Alec was starting to crack, Hazel was, too. He could see her getting a little defensive.

"Trust me, for you, they'll move mountains."

Hazel frowned at him. "They try, you know."

"Yeah, they try for *you*."

She set her jaw. "The only reason they do so much stuff for *me* is because they feel so guilty for worrying so much about *you*. Do you have any idea how much time Dad spent planning that camping trip?"

Alec did know, as a matter of fact. He'd listened to them from the top of the stairs as they orchestrated every detail of the trip in order to keep Alec calm. Like he was some sort of bomb they had to keep from going off.

His eyes drifted again to the bear. Alec got the strangest sensation, like he wanted to move their argument elsewhere.

Lonely Freddy, Alec thought to himself. *More like Nosy Freddy.*

Hazel put her hands on her hips. "I bet you didn't even know they moved here for you."

"What're you talking about?" Alec said, genuinely confused. His guard was slipping, but this was a turn in events he hadn't been expecting.

"The only reason we live here instead of our old house is because this one's closer to Aunt Gigi, and they think you like her more than you like them because she 'understands you,'" she said, twitching her fingers into air quotes.

"Well . . . ," Alec said, unable to argue. He did like his aunt better than his parents.

"Don't you think maybe that hurt their feelings a little bit?" she said, "For you to like mom's sister better?"

What was going on here? Where was all this anger coming from? Alec was so confused. Hazel was acting like . . . like . . . him!

"If they're so great and I'm so evil," Alec said, losing all sight of his Counter-Counterplan, "then why are you helping me and not them?"

Of all moments to clam up, Hazel did just that. She

recovered her facade faster than Alec did, which only worked
to infuriate Alec more. She'd somehow managed to gain the
upper hand despite his five years of experience on her.

"Hazel! Hazel, where are you?"

Hazel's green eyes stopped boring a hole through Alec
long enough to call to their mom.

"Coming!"

She turned on her heel and trotted around the corner
toward the party room, leaving Alec in the company of the
eavesdropping Freddy.

"What're you looking at?" he snarled at the bear, and he
had to suppress a chill because he swore he'd seen a reflection in the bear's eyes. Almost like a flash.

"Creeper," he said to it before loping down the same path
his sister had seconds before.

The Party Prepper was back with another question, and
their mom had reached peak decision burnout.

"Hazel, sweetie, do you want to have a chance at the
Wind Tunnel?"

She indicated to the large, tubelike enclosure with the
words WIND TUNNEL formed into the shape of a tornado
above the contraption. Inside, there were scraps of paper and
confetti left over from the last party. There were game tickets
and free toy coupons and glittery strips of cellophane confetti stuck to the inside of the tube.

"I don't care," she said, but it was such an obvious lie.
Alec wasn't fooled, and neither was their mom.

"But honey, you could have a chance at winning a Yarg Foxy. Isn't that what you want?"

"Wait, what?" Alec said, utterly betrayed. He couldn't help it. It was the ultimate betrayal.

Alec had never seen Hazel's face turn that shade of red. Her entire face and neck looked practically scalded. As though she could feel his stare through the back of her head, she whipped around to confirm that Alec had been witness to the whole exchange.

Oh, I saw, he thought. *The one thing, the* one thing *you knew I wanted.*

"Okay, I'll bite," said Aunt Gigi, interjecting just in time to clue in all of the uninitiated. "What's a Yarg Foxy?"

The Party Prepper merely pointed to the top level of the prize shelf, a huge red sign proclaiming its price: 10,000 tickets.

"It's that pirate fox," their mom said dismissively.

Aunt Gigi walked over to the prize shelf to try to get a closer look. "I don't get it," she said.

The Party Prepper sighed.

"I don't either," their mom said, "but kids go nuts for the thing."

Hazel looked down at the ground, her ears scarlet.

"Does it do anything?" Aunt Gigi said.

"It swings a hook," said their mom.

"Oh. Then what's the thing that follows kids around?" said Aunt Gigi, directing her question to their mom.

"Huh?"

"You know," Aunt Gigi said, snapping her fingers to try and trigger the memory. "The bear or whatever."

"Oh, right," their mom said, turning back to the Party Prepper, whose eyes were slow to leave her phone.

Then, without answering their mom's question, the prepper turned a dial on her hip-clipped walkie-talkie and pressed her finger to her headset.

"Someone get Daryl to do a Lonely Freddy demo."

They could hear the response from the headset even as she pressed it to her head. "Daryl's on break."

The prepper released a sigh so long, Alec wondered how she didn't pass out. Then, without a word, she crossed the restaurant toward a platform holding a familiar-looking, two-foot bear. The rest of them caught on after a minute and followed her like little quail.

The prepper bent her elbow and stationed her hand palm-up toward the bear that looked identical to the one Alec had stared down between the stage and the arcade. Same stock-straight posture. Same dead stare into the distance.

"This is a Lonely Freddy," the Party Prepper began, reading a script from memory in a tone somewhere between apathy and contempt.

"At Freddy Fazbear's, we believe that no child should have to experience the wonder and delight of Freddy Fazbear's Family Pizzeria alone. Using patented technology and a touch of that Freddy Fazbear magic, your child can engage in a getting-to-know-you session with the bear. Freddy will learn all about your child's favorite things, just like a true friend."

Aunt Gigi leaned close to their mom. "Is it just me, or does 'Lonely Freddy' sound like the cure for the unwanted kid?"

"Gigi!"

"Meg, seriously, it's a mechanical last resort. As in, no one wants to play with this kid, so here's a machine that'll do it instead."

The Party Prepper, close enough to hear, lifted an eyebrow but didn't argue.

Alec coughed and muttered, "Losers." But it was such a terrible act. If there was ever a kid who would have been foisted onto a Lonely Freddy at a birthday party, it would have been Alec. He might have known that if he'd ever been invited to one.

"For the safety of your children, we must ask that you refrain from climbing on, riding, or otherwise mistreating the Lonely Freddys. Parents and/or guardians assume full responsibility for the health and welfare of their children in the presence of this proprietary technology."

And with that, the Party Prepper's script came to a close, and she walked back toward the party room. The rest of them followed, the decision about the Wind Tunnel still left unmade. The Lonely Freddy detour had done nothing to resolve the question at hand, and they were trying the Party Prepper's last ounce of already depleted patience.

Aunt Gigi leaned into their mom and muttered, "Can't you just buy the fox and skip the drama? What if she doesn't get the winning coupon in that wind contraption?"

Their mom looked frantic. "It's not the same as *winning* it."

Hazel overheard their debate, and though Alec could tell she was trying to play it cool, Hazel's eyes kept darting back to the top shelf of the prize counter, where a brand-new Yarg Foxy sat in his box, ready to be taken home, underneath a bright red sign that said WIN ME IN THE WIND TUNNEL!

It was obvious she wanted the fox, so why was she pretending not to? Of course, all that mattered was that she wanted it.

And when you don't get it, everyone's going to see you for the spoiled phony you are.

Finally, Alec's Counter-Counterplan was coming together.

"Hazel, you should do the Wind Tunnel," he said to her in a voice carefully calibrated to just the right volume to be heard by both her and his mom.

Aunt Gigi cocked her head at Alec, then leaned back into their mom. "Did you switch to the organic milk?"

Their mother pinched the bridge of her nose like she did whenever she felt a migraine coming on, then turned to the Party Prepper.

"Just add the Wind Tunnel to the package," she said.

★　★　★

Back at home, Alec and Hazel kept up their new routine, with Alec playing the hero and Hazel playing the villain. Their mom pointedly ordered Alec to keep away from the freshly mopped kitchen floor, and Hazel responded by trekking across the tiles with muddy shoes. Their mom asked Alec to sort the recycling, and Hazel instead dumped the bottles and newspapers directly into the household garbage dumpster.

"Hazel, what on earth has gotten into you?" their mom finally broke, and Aunt Gigi watched in wide-eyed wonder as Hazel responded.

"I have no idea what you're talking about," she said, then scampered upstairs and slammed her bedroom door shut.

Alec took a seat on his usual step at the top of the stairs.

"It's like she's possessed!" their mom said.

"It's like she's *ten*," Aunt Gigi said, and Alec had to laugh because Aunt Gigi had no idea she was helping their little act along. The more their parents thought they were crazy, the more they'd be tempted to finally do away with all the parenting books and remember that Alec wasn't a problem to be solved. Or in this case, he supposed, Hazel.

"It's like they've switched places, Gigi. It's creepy!" their mom said.

"What's this?" Aunt Gigi said, but Alec couldn't see what she was referring to from his place on the stairs.

"It's just this book," their mom said, the exhaustion in her voice making it clear she'd lost her faith in *The Plan Planner*.

"Meg, you know I think it's great how you and Ian are always working to make sure you don't raise a couple of serial killers."

"Thanks, Gigi," their mom said dryly. "Glad to know our efforts are evident."

"I mean it. I think you guys are really good parents," said Aunt Gigi.

"I'm sensing a 'but' in there somewhere," their mom said.

"But, don't you ever wonder if in all your efforts to make them normal kids—whatever *that* means—if maybe you've . . ."

"If we've what?" their mom didn't sound so much defensive as petrified of the answer.

"Maybe you've made them what they are," Aunt Gigi said, pausing for a moment before adding: "Hazel's the easy one. Alec is the hard one. It's like you put them on their own little islands."

"Gigi, I love you," his mom said.

"I'm sensing a 'but' here," Aunt Gigi said.

"But if one more person tells me how to raise my kids, I'm gonna scream," his mom said.

To her credit, Aunt Gigi was silent after that.

"I just want us to be a family. An actual family," Alec's mom said, and he thought she'd never sounded more tired than she did right then.

"Congratulations," his aunt Gigi said dryly. "You are one."

As Alec stood to sneak off to his room, he heard his mom

laugh at Aunt Gigi's joke, though there was really nothing funny about it.

Just like Hazel, Alec's mom had everything she wanted, but she still wanted more. She wanted the perfect kids with the perfect manners in the perfect house. It wasn't enough for Hazel to have all the friends in the world and the most epic party every single year for her birthday. She had to have a stupid fox, too. Why? Because it's the one thing she didn't have in her spoiled life.

Well, Alec understood now. He saw his sister for the entitled, fake Hazel she really was, and she'd done her level best to make him out to be the spoiled one, all so he wouldn't ruin her stupid special party day.

Nice try, Sis, he thought, and he could feel an outer shell harden around his rapidly beating heart. *Nice try, but you're in for quite the surprise on party day.*

His Counter-Counterplan was in full swing.

Alec's parents were about to crack. Hazel had only been kidding that night she asked if Alec thought they would break them, but it seems her question was rooted in at least a little reality.

They were barely holding it together by Thursday. Alec and Hazel had tormented them to within an inch of their lives. Alec had brought home a "pet" wolf spider, and Hazel had set it free in their parents' bed. Alec "helpfully" ordered a pizza for dinner, but Hazel secretly added double anchovies under the cheese. A friendly game of charades initiated by Alec ended with their mom practically in tears as the word *GOAT* came up, and Hazel mimed "What Mom smells like!"

Friday was more of a blur, with their dad doing all he could to keep the peace the day before Hazel's party, even though neither of their parents were feeling particularly celebratory toward their Golden Hazel.

"It has to be hormonal or something," they could hear their dad say as Alec and Hazel eavesdropped from their perch at the top of the stairs. "She's probably nervous about making sure all her little friends have fun at the party."

"Ian, I woke up last night to a spider the size of my palm crawling through my hair," their mom said, her voice wavering as she neared tears for the umpteenth time that week.

"Oh man, I thought they found that yesterday," Alec whispered, and flinched as a stab of actual guilt hit his gut.

"They did," Hazel said. "I, um, re-rescued it."

Alec stared at this stranger he thought was his sister. His resolve toward exposing her may have doubled, but he couldn't deny he was genuinely impressed. He couldn't have thought up half the mini-disasters she'd set loose in their house over this past week. He found himself lamenting the return to their separate islands once this whole ruse was over. Regardless of the reasons or the double- and triple-crossing at play, he was going to miss her. He couldn't remember the last time he'd felt such a close camaraderie to this little stranger.

Maybe he couldn't remember because he'd never actually had one before.

Saturday morning, their parents did something they hadn't done in years: They let Alec and Hazel sleep for as long as they wanted. Hazel woke up much earlier than Alec, but she chose to stay in her room, playing quietly until Alec finally got up at nine o'clock.

As soon as his bedsprings creaked and he rose to sit on the edge of his bed, he heard Hazel's soft footsteps padding from her bedroom to his. The bathroom door creaked open, and she entered his room with a casualness that would have been unheard of seven days ago.

"Big day," Alec said, studying her face for a reaction.

He'd expected excitement, or smugness, maybe even a twinge of guilt at all the torture they'd put their parents through, a sort of practice she wasn't accustomed to, no matter how much she had decided she wanted to be a little less Golden.

He didn't see any of that in her face, though. He saw the usual evenly spaced freckles, the wide, light-green eyes, the perfect blonde ringlets that haloed her head. But there was something else. It was impossible to believe it was anything other than abject sadness.

"You're about to get everything you want," he said, scrutinizing her, but she gave nothing away.

"Yup," she said, though it was clear she didn't agree.

"You know, after this, you can probably go back to being nice, and they'll totally forgive you," he said.

He, on the other hand, could go back to being his usual rotten self after this, and he'd receive zero credit for having been decent to his family for the last week.

"Yeah, you're probably right," she said, taking a seat on the carpet beside his bed.

As she started to pick at the lint in the rug, Alec started to wonder if that's what she wanted, to go back to being the good one.

And he was surprised to find that regardless of what she wanted, that was what *he* wanted. All this plotting and counter-plotting was getting exhausting. He thought he could outplay his sister and protect his status as the bad egg, and maybe he still could. But what was it all for anyway? So he could keep himself exiled to his own little island in the house?

Had it really been that bad hanging out with her for the last week?

She started to stand up and walk toward the door, avoiding eye contact with Alec, and he found himself saying what he said next without even thinking.

"Happy birthday," he said, and this time, she did turn to look at him.

And she smiled. He thought it was real. He didn't want to think it was anything other than that. This morning had been very confusing.

★ ★ ★

The party was all the barely controlled chaos it had been in previous years. Kids standing on chairs rubbing balloons on one another's heads to create static. Parents calling out "Where's Jimmy? Has anyone seen Jimmy?" Freddy Fazbear staff expertly sidestepping spilled orange drink and fielding requests for more ranch dressing.

Amid the chaos, Alec could see one or two kids from the party walking around the restaurant with a two-foot Lonely Freddy in tow. It might have been cute if it hadn't been so creepy, watching this not-quite-tall but not-quite-short bear follow its "friend" around, listening and waiting for cues before acting autonomously. And Aunt Gigi's comment may have rung a little too true for Alec's comfort, but that day, he saw that truth in all its baldness—the kids who played too rough, whose noses crusted around the nostrils, whose faces twisted into sour frowns, were the ones followed by the bears and no one else.

Hazel wasn't quite the Golden Hazel she'd been in previous years, but she was more or less back to her old self. She politely thanked her friends for buying her the gifts she acted like she wasn't expecting. She helped her mom pass cake around to all the guests and her parents before taking a bite herself. She spent equal time with each kid who attended, making sure not to let anyone feel left out as they breezed from game to game in the arcade.

Alec sat in the corner and played his role of the sulking,

teenaged older brother. By all rights, if he'd wanted one, he easily could have earned his own Lonely Freddy.

In a strange turn of events, his parents seemed relieved to see everything return to its normal, inadequate existence. Whereas in previous years, they would have been urging him to go play with his sister, nudging him to smile, prodding him to help them drag the presents to the car, this year they seemed just fine with allowing him to slouch in a chair and scowl at the partygoers.

"I think it's all going pretty well, don't you?" his dad asked his mom and Aunt Gigi.

"Did anyone remind the staff that Charlotte can't have chocolate? I should probably go remind them," his mom said.

"It's going great," Aunt Gigi said, casting a sideways look at Alec, who simply shrugged.

Actually, it was going great. His sister was once again recognizable to their parents, the party only had an hour left until things were to wind down, and no one had gotten injured or poisoned. All in all, a notable success.

Except it wasn't a success. Alec hadn't been able to play his trump card yet. And he hadn't been able to play it because Hazel wasn't playing her part anymore.

She'd done everything: played Skee-Ball, fought zombies in the virtual reality battleground, shot about a million baskets, watched two full performances of the Freddy Fazbear band . . . Yet every time the Party Prepper had come into the room trying to convince her to head over to the Wind Tunnel to snag the coupon for her prize, she found a reason not to go in. Instead, she'd look toward Alec, as though in some sort of silent standoff, and say to the Party Prepper, "I don't know if I want to do that anymore."

"But honey, that's all you've been talking about for weeks is trying to win the Yarg Foxy," their mom would say, but every time, she would blow the Party Prepper off and run away to play some other game with her friends.

Aunt Gigi shrugged. "Maybe she doesn't want it anymore. Kids are fickle."

Alec had been so prepared. He'd snuck away when nobody was looking. He'd sifted through three full buckets of coupons, tickets, and confetti that clung to him like spiderwebs, until at last he'd found the single Yarg Foxy ticket in the materials meant for the Wind Tunnel. He'd pocketed the coupon and gone about his sulking way, and no one was the wiser.

But if Hazel wasn't going to take her turn in the Wind Tunnel, it was all for nothing.

Alec realized if he was going to expose her for the brat she was, he was going to have to take a more active role than he had been taking.

"Maybe she's afraid of being disappointed," he said to his mom, and his mom seemed to think that was a pretty reasonable idea.

"Alec, you two have been getting along so famously

lately. Maybe you should try to convince her. I'm just afraid she's going to leave today and regret not even trying."

"Sure thing, Mom," Alec said, laying it on a little thick, but it fooled his mom, and she nodded approvingly as he headed to the arcade to fetch his sister.

He found her by the Whack-a-Mole tables.

"Oh, Hazel, a word?" he said, pulling her by the elbow with a sappy smile while her friends distracted themselves. He found himself standing once again in the aisle between the Fazbear stage and the arcade. Only this time, there was no creepy bear to stare blankly off in the distance. The platform and bear had been removed, leaving only an impression on the carpet in front of the pillar.

"What gives?" Alec said once they were out of earshot.

"What do you mean?" she actually had the nerve to say, squirming out of his grip while she looked back to wave to her friends.

"I mean you're back to being perfect little Hazel, and Mom and Dad are catching on," he said, hoping she'd take the bait.

"What're you talking about? Mom and Dad are thrilled. Everything is back to normal."

She seemed mad at him for some reason, and he wondered for a second if she'd figured his plan out to expose her as a phony.

Which is maybe why he played his hand a little too aggressively.

"You know, the party's almost over. You're going to go home without your stupid toy if you don't get in that Wind Tunnel."

She shrugged, looking down. Her freckles practically disappeared under her flushed cheeks.

"Maybe I don't need the toy anymore," she said.

"Of course you do!" he said, unleashing the full magnitude of his anger. She was clearly doing everything she could to push him to his limit. "You're not gonna get everything you want forever. Soon, you're going to get older, and you won't be so precious, and then who's going to like you?"

In all of her ten years, outside of the infant months, Alec had never seen his sister cry. Maybe she had thrown a fit or two when she was a toddler, but he'd always found better places to be when that sort of drama went down.

But in that moment, for reasons he couldn't begin to understand, he watched as her light-green eyes rippled with tears. And though she wouldn't let them spill to her cheeks, he could tell it was a monumental effort on her part to keep them in.

"Fine," she said, and not a word more. She shoved past him and walked straight through her crowd of friends in the arcade toward the party room, greeting her mom and dad and aunt with nary a smile before demanding to be let into the Wind Tunnel.

"Oh . . . oh, yes! Okay!" their mom said, not the enthusiasm she'd been counting on, but she was quick to take action.

"She's ready for the Wind Tunnel!" she called out to the Freddy's staff like they were her ladies-in-waiting.

Two employees prepped the chamber by emptying the buckets of game tickets and coupons and sticky cellophane confetti into the top of the tube before flipping a switch to activate a strobe light that couldn't be looked at for too long without causing a touch of nausea.

Another flip of a switch, and the wind in the tunnel was activated, sending the assortment of paper and mylar whirling through the tube, mixing up the prize coupons in a dizzying frenzy.

They switched the machine off again, then rather unceremoniously grabbed Hazel by the wrists and pulled her through the little entrance door to the tube. The strobe lights reactivated, and as moths to a flickering flame, her friends migrated from arcade back into the party room to witness the birthday girl's tornado of potential prizes.

"Are. You. Ready??" asked an employee.

Hazel simply nodded, and Alec watched with measured awe as the storm kicked up around her, whipping her golden curls in front of her face and momentarily obscuring her behind the chaos.

"Grab the tickets!" her friends screamed from behind Alec.

"Oh! Oh, the Yarg Foxy coupon! It's right there, baby, it's right there!" his mom hollered, jumping up and down as though that could help. But Alec knew better. He touched the side of his jeans pocket where the single crinkled Yarg Foxy coupon resided.

Hazel barely reacted to the screams, though. She held her hands out haphazardly, making minimal attempts to grasp at any of the frenzied papers that flitted in and out of her fingers.

"Is she okay?" their dad asked, squinting into the chaos of the tube. "You don't think she's gonna puke, do you?"

"Oh boy, that would be a mess," Aunt Gigi said, and Alec had to stifle a snort.

"Come on, Hazel!" he shouted above the crowd, pretending to cheer along with them. "Get that certificate! Get that fox!"

But it was no use. Either she couldn't hear, or she simply didn't care.

When the Wind Tunnel timer buzzed, Freddy Fazbear associates dutifully pulled the plug, and the storm inside the enclosure came to an abrupt end.

"Okay, boys and girls!" the employee shouted into a microphone. "Let's see what the birthday girl has won!"

Kids from the party pushed and shoved toward the cylinder with Hazel inside it, and she sidestepped their greedy hands as they snatched at the free tickets like they were actual dollar bills.

"Well, Hannah, what've we got?" said the employee.

"It's Hazel," Aunt Gigi corrected.

"Okay!" said the employee, ignoring Aunt Gigi and

stepping dramatically over to Hazel as she cast him a wary look. "Let's see here!"

She handed him all the papers she had reluctantly grasped against her body, allowing him to sift through the various coupons and announce each one like she'd won the lottery.

"One free fountain drink! A bonus round at the Sky Dunk! One . . . no, make that *two* promotional Freddy Fazbear character cups!"

As the employee came to the end of the stack Hazel had captured, their mother started to shift nervously.

"She didn't get the fox," Alec heard her fret to their dad.

"Meg, relax. She doesn't even want it anymore."

"Yes, she does, Ian. She's just trying to be a big girl."

"Well, Hannah, that's quite a haul!" the employee said once he'd read off all the prizes.

"Hazel!" Aunt Gigi yelled, and this time the announcer looked over his shoulder long enough to cast her a sidelong glance.

"*Hazel,*" he corrected, grimacing at Aunt Gigi, who smiled her fakest smile back.

"Wait!" screamed the girl named Charlotte who couldn't eat chocolate. "Look in her hair!"

Sure enough, as her friends spun her to the side, Hazel's curls cradled a small glittery ticket that looked different than any of the others she'd managed to capture in the tunnel.

But Alec recognized it immediately.

"It's the Yarg Foxy! It's the Yarg Foxy!" screamed Charlotte.

It's not possible, Alec thought. Anger burbled in the pit of his stomach and began to churn, ready to erupt at any second.

He remembered the tube before the Wind Tunnel had turned on. There'd been little scraps in there from the last round. And in that small pile of glittery confetti and tickets, a single Yarg Foxy coupon must have been hiding, waiting to be kicked up again by a renewed wind.

Alec was certain she hadn't meant for it to, but Hazel's face completely transformed. It was only for a fraction of a second, but he was looking at her at just the right time. And in that split second, he saw her utter relief at having won the prize she was determined not to want when the day came to get it.

And no one would get to see the epic tantrum of Golden Hazel, the girl who had everything but didn't get the fox.

"That's right, boys and girls! Hazel has won her very own Yarg Foxy!" the announcer cried, and the kids from the party practically went into convulsions.

They followed the employee all the way to the prize counter and swarmed him as he lifted the boxed Yarg Foxy from the highest shelf, bestowing it upon Hazel like she'd just been crowned the queen.

"What a relief!" Their mom sighed, falling back into a chair.

Alec looked at her like she'd just grown a second head. A relief?

"It's a joke!" he said, and she scowled at Alec.

"How can you say that? You know how much she wanted that toy."

"Does she look like she wants the stupid toy?" he groused, still furious that Hazel was doing all she could to hide the fact that she was the spoiled one.

Alec watched as she unboxed the fox and held it in her hands, smiling at it like it was some sort of long forgotten treasure.

"Let me see, let me see!" her friends begged, but Hazel smiled shyly and shook her head.

"Honey, why don't you want to play with it?" their dad asked, and Hazel simply demurred. It wasn't until her friends had lost interest and migrated back toward the arcade that their mom finally pulled Hazel aside.

"Sweetie, what is it? Don't you want the fox anymore?" she asked, and Alec had just about had all he could take.

"Of course not! She gets everything she wants, and she's still not satisfied! But aw, isn't it sad that Hazel doesn't want the fox anymore?" Alec bellowed. He mocked. He sneered. But no one was listening.

That's when Hazel excused herself for a good long while. It had to have been at least ten minutes.

"I told you she was going to throw up," their dad said. "I'll go check on her."

But just as he was headed to the back room where Hazel had disappeared, she reappeared with the fox, still clutching it in her hands like it was suddenly very important to her after all.

"Hazel, sweetie, are you feeling okay?" their mom asked, stroking Hazel's curls, and suddenly, Hazel didn't look so glum or distracted (or nauseous, to hear their dad tell it). Instead, she leaned into her mom and whispered something that made their mom practically melt into a little puddle, right there on the Freddy Fazbear's floor.

Then their mom did something unexpected.

"Alec, come here, hon," she said, and Alec eyed them both suspiciously. To be fair, so did their dad and Aunt Gigi.

"Just come here," their mom said, rolling her eyes, but she was still smiling.

Alec approached his mom and sister with caution. He had the distinct impression he was walking into a trap.

"Go on, Hazel. Tell him what you told me," their mom said.

Hazel looked mortified. Her face was practically buried in the plush fox.

"Look at you. Shy as ever. Okay, I'll just be right over here," their mom cooed, and Alec was about to climb out of his skin.

"What the heck are you doing?" he whispered through gritted teeth. He was so close—so close—to beating his sister at her own game.

No, *his* own game. This was *his* to win.

"Nothing," she said. "I don't want to do this anymore."

"Do what?" Alec said, growing nervous. He looked up at his parents, but it didn't appear they'd heard anything.

"I don't want to pretend to be bad anymore. It was just to get you to like me."

Alec was speechless.

"Huh?"

"Here," she said, and shoved the Yarg Foxy into his chest. "It's for you."

"Aw, sweetie, look!" their mom said, and their dad shushed her, but their parents and Aunt Gigi continued to stare.

"You can't be serious," Alec said.

"I only wanted it so I could give it to you," she said.

"What the heck am I gonna do with a stupid fox?" he asked. No, he demanded. This was all just too much. How had she so expertly bested him?

"I wanted you to stop hating me so much. Just take it, okay?" she said, and shoved it into his chest.

None of this was working out the way it was supposed to. She was supposed to miss out on the fox, throw the epic fit he just knew she'd been storing up inside all week, and when his parents and all her friends saw her for the spoiled brat she really was, life should have gone back to the way Alec had enjoyed it before: with him to act in relative obscurity, without the burden of Golden Hazel's constant goodness.

But now, she had the fox, and what was she doing? She was giving it to him! In an act of utter sainthood, she was giving her most prized possession to him. She's won it *for him*. Because she knew how much *he'd* always wanted one.

She'd just checkmated.

"No," he said, flinging the fox back at her. "No, I don't want it."

"Alec! What sort of way is that to act toward your sister? She's giving you her gift *on her birthday!*" their mom cried.

"She's such a phony! Can't you people see that?? She's the worst kind of spoiled, bratty fake! How can you not see that?"

Alec was ranting now. It was all he could do to keep his head from spinning on his neck, *Exorcist*-style.

"You want me to take the fox?" he said, and he could only guess by the way his mother looked at him that he looked positively maniacal. "Okay fine, I'll take the fox."

He ripped the toy back from his sister's grasp hard enough to tear the arm, sending soft tufts of stuffing floating into the air.

Their mother let out an involuntary shriek, and Aunt Gigi put her hand on her sister's shoulder.

"Meg, get a grip. You're making it worse."

Their dad tried to make it better.

"Alec, come on, sport. Don't do this today."

"Oh, I see, because it's so predicable that Alec would ruin the party. It's so inevitable that Alec would spoil perfect little

Hazel's good time," he said, snarling at his family, who could only look back at him in horror.

All of them, that is, except for Hazel. Hazel simply stood there, arms limp at her sides as she stared at him.

And there they were. The tears.

She hadn't let them fall earlier. She had saved it all up for that moment, when she had the perfect audience. That's when she let the floodgates open. And even still, she only let a few fall.

"I can't take it anymore!" Alec raged, and carried by the wind of the truly possessed, he fled the scene of his worst crime yet. He'd brought the whole party crashing down around him, just as they'd all predicted he would. He'd done his very best to get the better of his sister, and in the end, she'd still won.

And if that wasn't enough, she'd actually made him believe—for the briefest moment—that she really was as good as she pretended to be. And that she'd wanted to be his friend.

Pounding a path through the pizzeria, Alec whizzed past confused-looking staff and his sister's gang of friends and one or two Lonely Freddy bears, barely registering any of it, including Hazel's friend, Charlotte, who was about to puke because someone had ignored all warnings to the contrary and fed her chocolate.

He didn't stop running until he'd pushed himself through at least three sets of doors and left the cacophony of kids and games and bells and singing behind him. He was somewhere in the cramped maze of backrooms that made up the inner workings of Freddy Fazbear's Family Pizzeria.

He slowed to a walk as he tried to catch his breath, but it wasn't until he'd come to a complete standstill that he realized why it was he couldn't seem to exhale. It was because he kept gulping air in.

It was because he was sobbing. Just like a little kid. Just like a spoiled brat.

He backed against a wall and threw his shoulders against it, once and then again, tucking his chin to his chest as he let his shoulders absorb all the shock.

"It's not my fault," he said, again and again. "It's not my fault."

But the more he heard his pathetic words in his ears, the more he knew they weren't true. It was his fault, all of it. He'd ruined the party, ruined Hazel, ruined his whole fifteen years by believing everyone was out to get him. He closed his eyes as he threw his shoulders again and again against the wall as he pictured Hazel's watery eyes, the lines creasing his mom's forehead, his dad's head shaking in disappointment.

Finally, he'd tired himself out enough to stop slamming against the wall, only to realize it wasn't a wall at all; it was a door. And what he'd thought was the sound of his own tantrum was actually a sound coming from the other side of the door, something that sounded like a loud thumping.

Pressing his head against the door for a closer listen, he looked up and down the hallway to make sure no one was coming before he ducked into the room with the strange sound.

The light switch was deep inside the room to his right, and he had to walk several steps in the dark, groping the wall until he finally found it, the door having closed with a heavy *thunk* just after he'd stepped inside.

When the room was finally lit, he saw it was something of a storage room, only far more cluttered with what appeared to be abandoned toys, arcade games, and machinery than the extra stocks of napkins and paper cups he was expecting. The back wall was lined with long-dormant arcade games Alec could remember being popular ten or so years ago. Folded cafeteria-style tables were stacked in rows against a side wall, their attached circular seats giving the arrangement a look like dominoes. The wall closest to him consisted of rows of wire racks, each holding various broken or dated toys that might once have been part of the prize counter display. Now, the cluttered shelves of sad, ownerless toys looked less like prizes and more like the stuff that goes missing under kids' beds.

He slumped into one of the seats of a cafeteria table that had fallen from its place against the wall.

His nose was still running from his meltdown in the hallway, and when he lifted his hand to drag it across his face, he felt a tickle of plush and remembered he was still holding the fox.

Its torn arm dangled by a few stubborn threads. Otherwise, the toy was shiny new, just as it had been promised to the kid lucky enough to get that stupid coupon.

"You weren't even supposed to *be* here," he said to the fox, but he couldn't muster the rage to give the words any bite. He was all angered out. In fact, he could hardly feel anything but the shame of having failed so miserably to show his sister up.

Her words rang in his ears: *I wanted you to stop hating me so much.*

This couldn't be it. This couldn't be what his sister had wanted this whole time—to win a toy he'd never gotten because good kids earned 10,000 ticket prizes and bad kids got followed around by a bear for a friend.

Alec held his head in his hands, hoping his mind would still. But memories of his sister came rushing back, crashing through his skull and ping-ponging off the insides of his brain like a dated arcade game.

The pictures she would draw for him and randomly slip under the crack of the bathroom door.

The dumb jokes he'd make that only she would laugh at.

The last piece of pumpkin pie she would never eat at Thanksgiving because she knew it was his favorite.

There were all the moments over the past week, times when he thought she'd been one-upping him, trying to outdo his cunning. Times when he'd thought he caught her looking at him but couldn't figure out what she was thinking. He'd just assumed she was scheming. But what if she was just looking? What if she was just waiting for him to look back at her?

What if she was just waiting for him to be a big brother?

Alec could barely form a cogent thought.

It seemed impossible that he'd gotten it all so wrong: the attention his parents lavished on her and spared for him; the bad seed label he'd given himself that he was so certain the family had given him; the days and months and years he'd spent lamenting his outsider-ness. What if they'd all actually wanted him inside with the rest of them?

He thought about what Hazel told him the other day, how she'd seemed so upset, and he couldn't figure out why.

I bet you didn't even know that we moved here for you.

She was trying to tell him, to get him to understand.

I wanted you to stop hating me so much.

Alec couldn't control himself. He clutched the pirate fox, squeezing the life it didn't have out of it before throwing it as hard as he could into the shelves beside him, knocking a bin of outdated, unwanted toys to the floor right along with the brand-new Yarg Foxy with the torn arm. All the toys fell in a collective heap to the floor, spilling across the dusty ground in various thumps and squeaks.

"Great," Alec said. "Just fantastic."

It wasn't enough he'd ruined the party and hurt Hazel,

but now he was going to get in trouble for trashing the back room of Freddy Fazbear's.

He ducked behind the shelving rack and began sifting through the toys, throwing them back into the bin they fell out of while doing his best to locate the fox. After everything he'd already done, losing the toy she gave to him just wasn't an option. Not if he ever had any hope of making things right.

But finding the Yarg Foxy proved to be a harder task than he'd thought it would be. There were rubber ducks and plastic snakes and felt puppets, but there was no peg-legged fox with a tragically torn arm.

"C'mon, seriously?" Alec said, exasperated and utterly exhausted by this time.

All he wanted was for this horrible day to be over with.

Alec was so lost in the sea of toys that he forgot about the thumping—that strange sound he'd heard on the other side of the door before pushing his way in. He hadn't heard it again since opening the door, but the thumping was back now, echoing from some part of the room he couldn't see. Now that he was behind the shelving unit, though, he could tell that the sound was coming from somewhere close by.

He peered into the far corner of the room, in a cluttered area behind the very last shelving unit lining the wall. There, tucked into a shadowy corner, was a large green Dumpster-type container, a padlock sealing the lid shut.

Alec took a few slow steps closer to the Dumpster, hoping

beyond hope that the thumping wasn't coming from inside that bin.

Now beside the bin, he hadn't heard any more thumping for the last several seconds, and he was mostly satisfied that he'd been mistaken. Clearly, the thumping had to be coming from the other side of the wall the Dumpster leaned against.

But just as Alec slid his fingers underneath the lid to peek through the crack allowed by the lock, the bin rattled and thumped, and he stumbled backward, scooting as far away from the container as he could get.

His heart pounded hard enough in his chest that he thought it might explode, but when nothing crawled out from under the crack in the lid, his pulse eventually began to slow to a normal pace.

Rats. It had to be rats, or some other sort of vermin.

"Glad I didn't eat the pizza," he said to himself and felt his stomach turn.

Leaning on his elbows, Alec found himself wedged between the wall and the farthest shelving unit from the door, buried behind a sea of forgotten things.

And there, staring at him from underneath a colorful canopy like something he might have seen in a circus, was a Lonely Freddy bear, just like the one he'd seen staring into nowhere that day he argued with Hazel.

"You again," he said to it. "You being punished or something?"

But he immediately disliked the thought of the already unsettling bear having . . . misbehaved.

He stared at the bear as it stood at attention on its platform under the canopy, seeming to gaze at something just over Alec's shoulder.

Alec turned and looked at the green Dumpster behind him, but when he turned back around, he was startled to find that the Lonely Freddy's eyes had somehow shifted.

They seemed to looking right at Alec.

"I've been waiting for you, friend," the bear said.

Alec stopped and stared at the bear.

"Um, that's great," he said to it, and that should have been the end of it.

Alec didn't expect it to say something else.

"We should be best friends."

"What?" Alec said, looking a little harder at the bear. Was this how it was supposed to work? He thought it was supposed to be sort of interviewing him. But the bear wasn't asking him questions so much as it was . . . telling him things.

"Very best friends," said the bear.

"Okay," Alec said, trying to brush off the chill that kept running up his arm.

It's a stuffed animal, he said to himself. *It's a stupid toy.*

But it was strange that no matter how many times he tried, Alec couldn't seem to stand up. He couldn't seem to

look away from the bear. All he could do was sit there and
stare at it as it stared back.

Alec had never noticed the bear's eyes before. Had they
always been that blue? And if he didn't know better, he'd
think that they were almost glowing. But that was crazy.

Then it did start to ask him questions.

"What's your favorite color?"

"My favorite color?" Alec asked, almost as if he wasn't
in control of his own voice anymore. "My favorite color is
green."

The bear moved immediately to the next question. Wasn't
it supposed to share things about it, too?

"What's your favorite food?"

"Lasagna," said Alec, his answer automatic and immediate.

"What do you want to be when you grow up?"

"A pro skateboarder."

"What's your best subject in school?"

"History."

It went on like that for what felt to Alec like hours, but it
couldn't possibly have been that long. He was having such a
hard time feeling the floor underneath him or the sensation
in his fingers. It was like he was floating, like he was hearing
every question drift to him from the end of a long tunnel.

Then the bear's questions took a different turn.

"Who do you admire most?"

"My aunt Gigi."

"What do you fear the most?"

"The dark."

"What would you do if you were asked to hurt someone you love?"

It felt like the bear was reaching its soft, plush paw into his very soul and extracting the answers he kept the most hidden. And it was doing it so effortlessly.

Its eyes were as blue and deep as an ocean trench.

"What's your biggest regret?"

And at this question, Alec did stop. He resisted at first, or maybe he simply didn't know the answer. But the bear wouldn't move on. It asked again.

"What's your biggest regret?"

Still, Alec hesitated, and the pull from inside of him began to grow painful, like something was squeezing him from his very core.

"What is your biggest regret . . . Alec?"

With the pressure building from inside, he could barely breathe against the pain, and through the tiny spaces in his gritted teeth, the answer trickled out.

"Hurting Hazel."

The pressure eased, and sensation eventually returned to Alec's body, warming his extremities all the way to the middle of him. But when his body breathed back to life, something felt fundamentally different.

He stared hard into the blue eyes that had burned through his soul, and he searched for answers of his own, but he only came away with more questions because the blue eyes of the bear had suddenly turned light green.

"What's happening?" he tried to ask the bear, because suddenly, the bear seemed to be the one with all the answers, but Alec couldn't open his mouth.

He stared and he stared, and the bear simply stared back.

A panicky feeling began to rise in his chest.

I just need to get outside, he thought. *I need some air.*

But breathing wasn't his problem. Moving was.

He tried to extend his leg to stand, but nothing happened. He wanted to push his palm to the floor to brace himself, but he couldn't.

Voices, faint at first but growing louder as they approached, gave him a touch of renewed hope. He recognized them immediately.

"Mom! Hazel!" he called out, or at least he tried, but every time he felt his throat flex to yell, the words struggled to find their way out.

"Don't worry, sweetie, we'll find it," he could hear his mom say.

The thumping from the giant bin behind him kicked up again, and he wanted so badly to move away from it, but nothing was working. Every muscle suddenly felt crystalized.

"Did you hear that?" Alec heard Hazel say from the other side of the door.

Yes! Screamed Alec. *In here! Look in here!*

He could hear the door open from the other side of the room, but he couldn't see around the shelving unit. All he could see was the bear as its newly green eyes bore through him.

"I don't think we're supposed to be in here," Alec's mom said, and he thought he'd never been more relieved to hear her voice.

"Mom, look!" said Hazel.

For a second, Alec's heart leapt. They'd spotted him. He couldn't see them, but maybe they saw him.

What if I'm having some sort of seizure? he thought.

No matter, though. His mom and his sister were here to help now.

Except why weren't they talking to him? Why hadn't they come around the side of the shelving unit?

"Aw, see?" his mom said. "I told you we'd find it."

But you haven't found me! Alec tried desperately to scream. *I'm right here! I'm right here!*

The thumping from the bin had gone silent the moment the door opened, and why now? Why couldn't the noise pick up again now?

"He just . . . threw it in here," Hazel said, and the pain in her voice was enough to make Alec feel like the smallest, most disgusting cockroach.

"Hazel," their mom said, her voice so gentle. "He loves you. I know he does. In his own way, he really does love him. Just like we love him."

Alec's throat tightened into a knot, and this was the moment. This was finally the moment he would tell them how sorry he was, how wrong he was, how much he'd missed out on by wanting so badly to believe he was on the outside.

Now all he felt was that he was somehow trapped . . . *inside*.

"Come on, sweets. The party is going to wrap up soon. Let's go polish off that cake, shall we?"

"Hang on," Hazel said.

Please see me, Alec silently pleaded. *See me*.

"Oh, don't worry about the arm, hon. I can fix that when we get home," said their mom.

Then he heard the worst sound. He heard Hazel choke on a sob.

"Oh, honey . . . ," their mom said.

"He hates me," said Hazel.

"He doesn't hate you. He's never hated you."

That was the thing, though. Alec *had* hated her. It was the worst, most awful confession he never made, but he didn't have to, because his sister had known all along.

What she didn't know—what he hadn't told her when he should have—was that he didn't hate her anymore. If he was telling his own deepest, darkest secret, he'd have told her that he hated himself far more than he ever hated her.

And he'd liked himself more this past week than he had

since the day she was born, and it was because he'd spent it plotting with her.

"C'mon," their mom said, and he could practically hear her squeezing Hazel's shoulder. "This will blow over. These things always do. Let's not let it ruin your birthday."

No. No! Alec tried to scream. *Don't leave me! I can't move!*

But it was no use. No matter how loud the voice was in his head, he couldn't push the sound from his throat.

Panic was rising at the base of his skull, and he was beginning to wonder what would happen if nobody came back here to look for him. Would they simply go home without him? Would anyone even miss him?

Alec stared hard into the now-green eyes of the bear and mustered every ounce of strength he could find in his core. It seemed to take everything he had, but suddenly, the bear before him was gone, hiding on the other side of Alec's closed eyes.

He'd figured out how to close his eyes.

Good, now breathe. Just count to ten and keep breathing, he told himself.

He pulled a deep breath in through his nose, out through his mouth, and repeated the exercise ten times, and just as he reached the tenth exhale, he felt the tips of his fingers twitch.

He was so excited, he opened his eyes, and he was stunned to find himself very much alone behind the shelving unit.

The bear was gone, its custom platform empty.

Where . . . ?

But he didn't have time to think about that now. He had just regained the tiniest bit of movement in his fingertips, and he wasn't about to stop there. He closed his eyes once again and repeated the breathing, hoping it would do the trick again. Sure enough, as he reached ten, he found with great relief that he was able to wiggle his big toe.

He repeated the exercise over and over, re-teaching his body how to move, and pretty soon, he could bend his knees and his elbows and even turn his head.

The thumping in the bin behind him started up again, and he was suddenly furious that the sound returned now when it was too late to do him any good.

Oh, shut up.

Unfortunately, even though his limbs had begun to cooperate, his voice still hadn't returned, nor had his ability to even open his mouth.

No time to worry about that now, he thought.

He was starting to feel his motor function come back online, perhaps a bit clumsily, but so long as he could eventually get himself to stand, that's all that really mattered. Surely once his parents and Aunt Gigi saw him, they'd see he was in need of help. He simply had to get out of this back room.

It seemed like he had to squeeze every muscle in his body in order to get his feet under him. He continued to close his eyes and breathe, taking encouragement from the small victories: leg bent, leg tucked, body balanced, other leg bent.

And though it took forever, at long last, he managed to stand straight on two legs.

The strangest thing, though, was that it almost seemed like he was still sitting. The shelf seemed so much higher than it had initially. In fact, the entire room looked bigger somehow, like the ceiling had risen.

He moved stiffly at first, his legs jerking more than walking, and he had to work extraordinarily hard to get control of them, but after several steps and as many pauses, Alec managed to find a rhythm adequate enough to move him to the other end of the room.

But when he came upon the door, he was stunned to find that he couldn't reach the handle. It was at least a foot above his head.

What?

Using the same practice he'd employed to get his legs working, he closed his eyes and took several deep breaths, and eventually, he was able to raise his hands high enough over his head to wiggle the handle of the door.

He pushed through the door after managing to nudge the handle enough to open it, and when he stumbled into the hallway, Alec again had to do a double take to make sure he was in the right place to find his way back out to the restaurant.

The hallway was much longer than it had been before. It seemed almost endless, and he felt so small inside of it.

But Alec pushed on. He only had to get back to the party

room. He only had to make his way back to his family. They would know what was wrong. They would know how to help him.

The end of the hallway was blocked by yet another door he'd remembered being much less of an obstacle. The handle was even higher here than it had been in the storage room, and no matter how high he stretched his arms into the air, he couldn't reach the lever that would let him back into the restaurant.

Don't panic, he told himself. *Someone is bound to come back here at some point.*

He had to wait a lot longer than he thought he would. Slumped against the wall to the side of the door, Alec tried not to let his mind wander too far. He was afraid he'd slip back into the trance he'd somehow fallen into in the storage room.

The way that bear had gotten into his head . . . there was nothing natural about it. He wasn't sure what or how, but something had happened to him, something horrible.

He just hoped it wasn't irreversible.

He hoped a lot of what happened today could be reversed.

All of a sudden, the door swung wide, nearly crushing Alec behind it, and he had to throw himself through the opening before the door slammed shut again.

Nose on the floor of the Freddy Fazbear carpet, he was again surrounded by the piercing screams and jangling game bells of the arcade.

The second Alec landed on the floor, he felt the wind knocked squarely out of him.

"GOOOOAAAAAALLLL!" he heard someone call, and then he heard others laugh, but that was all as he soared through the air, still trying to find his breath.

He landed with a painful thud, this time faceup and staring at the etched glass lampshades that covered each of the tables in the pizzeria. Feet pounded all around him, dangerously close to his head, and he winced as sneaker after sneaker narrowly missed squashing some part of him.

Why is everyone acting like they don't see me?

No sooner had the thought occurred to him than he was grabbed roughly by the arm and clutched tightly into an itchy wool vest.

"I saw it first!" said a voice, and suddenly, someone was tugging hard on his leg.

"No, I called dibs!" said the kid holding him, and how big were these kids that they were able to play tug of war with him?

"No me!"

"Me!!"

His leg was being pulled so hard, he was terrified it might come off any second. He wanted to go back to not being seen.

Then, just as quickly as the tug of war had started, a voice in the distance yelled "Pizza's here!" and he was again dropped onto the carpet.

He lay there on his side trying to recover himself, but a stroller wheel wobbled straight for his head, and he squeezed his eyes shut as he awaited certain death.

"Jacob, move that thing out of the way, would you?" said the person behind the stroller, and someone nudged Alec with their foot, wedging him against the baseboard.

Move that thing? Alec thought, and if he weren't so out-of-his-mind confused and in a fair amount of pain, he might have been offended.

He managed to brace himself against the wall and get to his feet, but he was so wobbly, he wasn't sure he'd be able to make it across the room without falling over.

Still, he was determined. He had to make it back to the party room. He just had to make it back to his family. Surely they'd be looking for him by now, wouldn't they?

Alec wobbled and weaved across the eatery, dodging stomping feet and spilled colas, getting sprinkled with Parmesan and crushed peppers from tableside shakers. After several near-death experiences, Alec found his way to the other side of the cavernous room amid the throngs of kids and families.

As he rounded the corner, he spied the enormous cylindrical tube that made up the Wind Tunnel, now dormant and awaiting the next birthday kid once Hazel's party was over.

Then there was his family—his mom in her dark jeans and his dad in his comfiest corduroy slacks and his flannel shirt, Aunt Gigi with her hair pulled back in her headband.

And there was Hazel, her blonde ringlets hanging in front of her face but still not obscuring the smile that couldn't help but light up the room. Her friends were leaning back in their chairs, rubbing their full bellies and rifling through goodie bags as they waited for their parents to pick them up.

They all looked so happy. Hazel especially beamed. It was like someone had switched the light on inside of her again. She was all at once relieved of the burden Alec had placed on her by being . . . himself. Except not the self he wanted to be, not anymore. He wanted to be the reason she would smile like that more often. He was ready.

That's when Alec saw that, in fact, he *was* the reason she was beaming.

There, sitting across the table from his sister and their parents, was . . . Alec.

It was the same rumpled T-shirt he'd thrown on that morning before the party, the same ripped jeans. The same unruly golden curls that provided the counterbalance to Hazel's perfect ringlets. It was his light-green eyes, his slightly crooked teeth, his lanky limbs.

And he was smiling. Smiling right back at Hazel.

Hey, Alec said, the voice in his head quiet at first, but quickly, it was screaming.

Hey! That's not me! That's not me!

But anyone looking at the kid across from Hazel would beg to differ. In every way, this person was most certainly him. Those questioning it might point to the fact that he wasn't sulking like the Alec they knew. He wasn't glowering at his sister the way he was known to do more often than not.

But he had seemed to be making an effort all week to turn over a new leaf, hadn't he? His parents had been trying this new technique, a method endorsed by a reputable doctor and best-selling author. Some kids just took longer to come into their own.

Wasn't it nice that Alec had managed to do just that, and on his sister's birthday of all days? How sweet. How perfect.

What a family they were turning out to be.

Alec forced his stiff legs forward and tumbled into the party room, but he could barely see above the table when he got inside. He thought maybe he could try climbing one of the table legs, but it was too slick.

He moved from kid to kid crowding around the table, doing whatever he could to attract the attention of just one of them. He had to get on top of that table. He had to look into his mom's eyes. She'd have to recognize him then, wouldn't she? Of course she would!

Look down! Someone please just look down! His mind screamed, but just as before, his throat refused to release his pleas.

It's a bad dream. This has to be some crazy, elaborate nightmare.

But it didn't feel like a nightmare. In fact, nothing had ever felt more real in his entire fifteen years.

He spied the girl called Charlotte sitting curled up in a

chair in the corner, clutching her stomach. She was the only kid not talking to someone else. She was his best chance at attracting attention.

But as he waved his arms to try and flag her interest, she turned suddenly and spewed all over his head, warm vomit dripping into his eyes and running down his face.

"Oh! Oh no, Charlotte, honey, is your stomach still bothering you?"

Alec could barely see through the puke pouring in rivers over his eyes, but the sound of his mom's voice was such a relief. In a minute, this whole insane day would come to an end, and he'd be able to rejoin his family.

"Oh, gross!" someone shouted, and to his horror, it was his own sister. "She puked on one of the bears!"

Wait, what?

"Hold on, I'll get one of the staff to come and clean it up," their dad said.

"Here, let me help," Aunt Gigi said, and he watched from his periphery as beautiful, wonderful Aunt Gigi hurried to his corner of the room.

Thank you, he whimpered in his head. His aunt Gigi would know what to do.

But instead of coming to Alec's aid, Aunt Gigi gently pulled Charlotte from her chair and sat her on the bench closer to Hazel and the fake Alec, who passed napkins to her so she could clean herself up.

"Have some water," Hazel said, offering her a cup.

"Here, you got some in your hair," the fake Alec said.

Then he turned to Alec. His eyes—his stolen green eyes in his stolen body—gleamed at Alec as he stood in the corner, dripping in vomit, watching his family welcome him into their fold.

And then the fake Alec smiled.

"Yes, just over here. Sorry. I think we ruined one of your bears," Alec heard his dad say from outside of the room, and just then, a Freddy's employee arrived with a mop and bucket.

"Not a problem, sir. We'll take care of this mess. You just go back to enjoying your party."

And with that, Alec was tossed into a bucket and rolled away, his vision still obscured, but not too much that he didn't see the fake Alec wink at him from the table before returning his attention to a smiling, laughing Hazel with her smiling, happy family.

In the bucket, Alec was quickly rolled to the back of the pizzeria once again, the doors he'd worked so hard to move thrust open and shut with ease by the employee. He made a quick stop in the men's room, where he shoved the wheeled bucket and mop into the corner and rung out the rag in the maintenance sink before slopping it over the side of the bucket, flecking the mirror beside them with large droplets of water.

Alec turned slowly to the mirror he only then realized he was parked beside.

There in the reflection stared a blue-eyed, two-foot Freddy Fazbear, its hair matted and starting to crust over with puke, its arms extended and ready for a hug.

This can't be. This can't possibly be.

But Alec had no time to contemplate what it was and what it wasn't. Before he knew it, they were on the move again.

The employee pinched Alec's paw between two fingers.

"Yick," he said, scrunching up his nose before holding Alec as far in front of him as he could. "Into the bin for you," he said.

He kicked open the men's room door and traveled quickly down the hall to the storage room Alec had escaped to earlier.

Wait, he tried to say. *Wait!*

But as ever, it was no use.

The employee pulled a collection of keys from a retractable cord on his belt loop as he made his way to the very back of the storage room toward a familiar, large green Dumpster.

"Which one is it?" he muttered to himself before landing on the right one. "Aha! Here it is."

Then the employee stuck the key in the padlock over the bin's lid, and with a sharp turn to the left, the padlock sprang open.

"Have fun with your little buddies!" he said, and released his pinch on Alec's paw, sending him falling through the air and into the bin.

The light from the room illuminated his surroundings in the bin long enough for Alec to see why it hadn't hurt when he fell in. His fall had been broken by dozens of plush bears that looked exactly like him.

Dozens of discarded Lonely Freddys.

"Nighty night," the employee said, and just like that, the light above him extinguished with the closing and locking of the lid.

Panic seeped into Alec's pores . . . or what might have once been pores.

In his head, he screamed and he screamed. But in the end, the only sound that crept from his unhinged, stuffed bear mouth was the tiniest squeak.

"Help!" he thought he heard himself say.

Then he realized it hadn't been him at all. It had been the bear beside him in the bin.

Then it was the bear on the other side of him.

Pretty soon, it was every bear in the bin, their thin, muted screams for help swallowed by the metal and darkness that entombed them. Alec and his new friends.

Dozens of the lonely ones.

OUT OF
STOCK

It was just like Oscar to be on the losing end of the deal.

It had always been that way, from the time his dad went to the hospital for a tonsillectomy and contracted a fatal infection, to the time that they had to move to the cheaper end of town, to all the times Oscar had to help his mom at the Royal Oaks Nursing Home while the rest of his friends spent their allowances at the mall.

So it was no surprise to Oscar when he learned that the Plushtrap Chaser—a light-activated chomping green rabbit, and by far Oscar's favorite character from the Freddy Fazbear world—would go on sale on the most ridiculous day, at the most ridiculous time imaginable.

"Friday morning. *Friday morning!*" Oscar steamed.

"Man, you've gotta get over it," said Raj, kicking the same stone down the sidewalk he'd been torturing the entire

"But the *injustice* of it!" Oscar said. "It's a kids' toy. Why would it go on sale when every kid in the known universe is in school?"

Oscar swatted at a low-hanging tree branch like it wronged him.

"Did you hear Dwight already got one?" Isaac asked, bringing up the rear.

"What?" Raj stopped for a minute, now adequately outraged. "He hadn't even *heard* of Freddy Fazbear before last year!"

"Apparently his dad 'made a call.' His dad's always 'making a call,'" pouted Isaac.

"Dwight's a jerk," said Raj, and on this, the boys all agreed. It was so much easier to hate Dwight than to admit they weren't the types who had dads who could make calls to get ugly green rabbits that stood the height of a toddler and maintained the speed of an actual rabbit.

"We'll never get it, not if we have to wait until four o'clock," Isaac said.

"We could—" Oscar started, but Raj cut him off.

"No, we can't," he said.

"How do you—?"

"We can't ditch."

"Maybe I—"

"It's not possible. I have two strikes already. One more, and my mom's going to send me to boot camp."

"C'mon, she wasn't serious about that," Oscar said.

"You don't know my mom," said Raj. "One time, my sister talked back to her, and my mom wouldn't let her talk for a week."

"That didn't actually happen," Isaac chuckled.

"Oh no? Ask Avni. She says by the sixth day, it's like she forgot how to talk at all."

Raj looked in the distance, haunted by the specter of his mother while Oscar turned to Isaac.

"Don't look at me. I have to walk Jordan home."

Oscar knew he couldn't argue with that one. Even as little brothers go, Jordan was okay, and Oscar knew for a fact that Isaac's mom would go nuclear if he even *thought* about leaving Jordan alone until she got home from work at three o'clock.

There was no getting around it. Despite all of Oscar's big ideas, he knew he was too afraid to actually go through with it. Ditching school was like a mortal sin to his mom, who'd fought hard for her own education while raising Oscar by herself.

Oscar and his friends would have to wait until four o'clock.

The day was agonizingly long. Mr. Tallis made the entire class recite the preamble of the Constitution over and over until they got it right. Ms. Davni popped a completely unfair quiz on isotopes. Coach Riggins made them run laps around the field even though it was still muddy from the last rain. Oscar thought maybe he'd never faced a more miserable day.

Then at 2:33, it got worse.

Two minutes before the final bell rang, Oscar was called to the front office.

"Now?" he pleaded with Mr. Enriquez.

His geometry teacher shrugged, helpless to bail Oscar out, despite his being Oscar's favorite teacher.

"Sorry, Mr. Avila. Nobody ever said sophomore year was cruelty free."

He turned to Raj and Isaac in the only class they'd ever shared since they met on the playground in the third grade.

Mustering all his strength, he tried not to choke on his sacrificial offering: "Wait for me until three thirty. If I'm not back by then . . ."

The whole class sat in witness.

". . . then go without me."

Raj and Isaac nodded solemnly, and Oscar scooped up his notebooks and bag and cast one last glance at Mr. Enriquez.

"It's your mom," he murmured, patting Oscar firmly on the shoulder. Mr. Enriquez knew Oscar's mom sometimes needed Oscar's help at the Royal Oaks Nursing Home. He didn't know exactly what his mom's job was, but it had something to do with making sure the whole place didn't come undone. His mom was important.

The secretary at the front desk was waiting impatiently for Oscar, the receiver already in hand.

"Thought you got lost," she said humorlessly. "Does your

mom know this is why most parents get their kids cell phones?"

Oscar bared his teeth into something simulating a smile. "I think she just likes hearing your voice on the regular," he said, and the secretary matched his smile. "Besides, phones aren't allowed at school."

Not that we can afford one, he thought, not without a little venom toward the secretary.

Oscar took the phone from her hand fast because she looked like she was about to smack him with it.

"LM, Mr. Devereaux isn't doing well today," Oscar's mom said. His mom only used his nickname, "LM," code for "Little Man," when her need was dire.

Not this. Not today. Mr. Devereaux was possibly the world's oldest man, and when he was out of sorts, there were only a few people who could reason with him enough to get him to take his meds or eat something. For some inexplicable reason, Oscar was one of those people.

"Where's Connie?" Oscar whined, referencing the only orderly to whom Mr. Devereaux responded.

"Puerta Vallarta, where I should be," his mom said. "Besides, he's asking for you."

Oscar handed the phone back to the secretary, who already had her purse in hand as she tapped her white-tipped fingernail on the counter between them.

"I trust you've resolved your crisis? I have to get to the Toy Box before they sell out of Plushtraps. I have five nephews."

It was almost too much for Oscar to bear. Five fewer Plushtraps after Ms. Bestly (Ms. *Beastly* in his head) snagged whatever might be left for her undeserving nephews. Oscar dragged his feet in misery all the way to the number 12 city bus, transferred to the 56 line, and walked the quarter mile from the bus stop to his mom's work, moping into the lobby of the Royal Oaks Nursing Home.

Irvin, seated at the reception desk, nodded to him from under his headphones.

"Dude's in a bad way, big man!" Irvin said loudly, his volume unchecked by the deep baseline emanating from his playlist. "He says Marilyn wants to steal his soul!"

Oscar nodded. Irvin was well-versed in the oddities of Royal Oaks, including Mr. Devereaux's chronic, baseless paranoia. Hearing Irvin confirm what his mom had already told him on the phone did nothing to alter Oscar's position of unconditional surrender. He would be here all afternoon, likely into the evening, trying to calm Mr. Devereaux. The Plushtrap Chaser, if he'd ever had a chance at getting it in the first place, would never be his now.

The automatic doors whooshed open, revealing the back of his mom's tall figure. She handed a clipboard back to an orderly Oscar hadn't met before. This place went through orderlies like Oscar went through Electric Blue Fruit Punch.

"Make sure Ms. Delia doesn't get any dairy after four p.m.," his mom said. "She'll fart so much, we'll have to quarantine the room, and I promise you, I'll make sure you're the only one assigned to that wing for the entire night."

The new orderly nodded earnestly, clearly shaken, and hurried away with the clipboard just as Oscar's mom turned to smile at him, arms extended. That was the thing about his mom—she could always be counted on for a hug strong enough to crack ribs. Even the time she threatened to put a bounty on Oscar's head after he "rescued" a bat and set it free in the house, she still managed to hug him hard enough to make him sore the next day.

"Mr. Devereaux thinks Marilyn—"

"—wants to steal his soul. I heard," Oscar said.

"After eighteen years, you'd think Marilyn had earned the benefit of the doubt."

"No rest for the truly suspicious," Oscar said, and his mom smiled at him.

"Thank you, Little Man. You are my angel."

"Mom," he said, looking around to make sure no one heard, even though the only ones who would give him a hard time were miles away at the Toy Box, claiming the very last Plushtrap no doubt. The thought of Raj and Isaac lining them up for epic, chomping battles in the yard was pure agony.

Oscar began to think about compromises. Maybe if he gave Raj or Isaac half the amount, one of them could be persuaded to let him take partial Plushtrap custody.

Oscar managed a weak smile at his mom and wondered if

the fates might bestow upon him a Plushtrap if they witnessed his angelic behavior. He knew better than to hope, though.

When he arrived in Mr. Devereaux's doorway, he found the old man staring into the corner of his room, his eyes trained like lasers ready to vaporize.

"It's started," Mr. Devereaux said, his voice barely above a whisper.

"What's started?" Oscar asked, not so much curious as eager to begin this process.

"She's been plotting this whole time. I should have known. She waited until I let my guard down."

"C'mon, Mr. D., you don't really believe that."

"I can feel my soul slipping away. It's oozing out of my pores, Oscar."

Mr. Devereaux didn't sound afraid; rather, he seemed resigned to his fate, and Oscar thought maybe they had something in common today.

"But why would she do that?" Oscar asked. "She loves you. She's shared your room every night for almost two decades. Don't you think if she wanted your soul, she would have taken it by now?"

"Trust cannot be rushed, young man," Mr. Devereaux said. "Good fortune cannot be predicted."

It was these seeds of wisdom that kept Oscar interested in Royal Oaks's longest-term resident. No matter how many times Mr. Devereaux let some sage observation slip, Oscar was surprised every time, like Mr. Devereaux could sense what was occupying Oscar's mind . . . even if Mr. Devereaux's own mind was like a sieve, his thoughts slipping through holes into some bottomless abyss.

"Maybe Marilyn isn't stealing your soul. Maybe she's guarding it. You know, like holding it for safekeeping," Oscar posited.

Mr. Devereaux shook his head. "I thought of that. It's a tempting theory . . . but she should have asked permission."

These are the times when Oscar struggled, when logic had to win.

"I mean, it's not like she can actually ask you," he said.

"Of course she can!" Mr. Devereaux raged, and Oscar put up his hands, trying to ease Mr. Devereaux before the new orderly came scurrying around the corner.

"Okay, but just stick with me for a minute, Mr. D.," Oscar said, sneaking two steps into Mr. Devereaux's room. "Maybe she thought, you know, since you were close enough, that you wouldn't mind if she . . . uh . . . *borrowed* your soul for a bit—"

Mr. Devereaux cut his eyes toward Oscar, suspicious.

"She didn't tell you to say that, did she?"

"No! No no no of course not. No one could come close to the, er, relationship you have."

Mr. Devereaux looked into the corner of the room that had held his attention until that moment.

"Well, Marilyn, what'd'ya have to say for yourself?"

Oscar followed Mr. Devereaux's stare, and now they were both staring at the same ancient calico cat who had slept on the pillow by the window of Mr. Devereaux's room for as long as Mr. Devereux had slept in his own bed. She didn't come here with Mr. Devereaux, at least according to legend. She'd been a neighborhood stray. But one day, the staff found her in the room, and without objection from the rotating cast of residents, Marilyn had remained, finding Mr. Devereaux's company the most pleasing, despite his periodic disdain or downright hatred. No amount of scratching behind the ears or catnip offerings by anyone else could entice her away from Mr. Devereaux.

Maybe she really *was* after his soul.

Marilyn blinked her slow cat blink at Mr. Devereaux.

"Well, I think we both know what that means," Oscar improvised, and for a second, Mr. Devereaux looked confused, but after another moment of contemplation over the loud purring of Marilyn, something inside him settled.

"All right then. It seems Marilyn owes you yet another debt of gratitude, young man."

Marilyn stretched languidly on her chair and yawned, but Oscar wasn't looking for gratitude from a cat. He was looking for a way out.

"Sit down, young man, sit down," Mr. Devereaux said, and Oscar let the last of his hope slip away. This was to be his entire afternoon.

Oscar slumped in the chair closest to the door.

Mr. Devereaux stared at him with the watery eyes of an old man.

"My soul may be in trouble," he said, "but your heart is stolen."

Oscar tried to laugh. If he didn't, he might cry. It was just the latest in what was panning out to be a lifetime of *almost*. He had *almost* made Varsity baseball, but he dislocated his elbow. He had *almost* saved enough for a cell phone, but someone picked his pocket on the train. He had *almost* had a whole family, but then he lost his dad.

If you could earn a trophy for *almost*, he'd probably fall just shy of the honor.

"Ah yes," Mr. Devereaux continued. "Love is a many splendored thing . . . until it crushes you to pieces."

"It's not like that," Oscar said. It was ridiculous to set the record straight; Mr. Devereaux might or might not even remember this conversation. But he needed someone to know, needed someone to confide in, and truly he had never known a better listener than this man whom he had never once seen standing, whose first name he didn't even know.

"It's . . . just this stupid toy," Oscar said, but even as he tried to diminish the Plushtrap, he felt his heart squeeze.

"It broke?" Mr. Devereaux said.

"It was never even mine," said Oscar, and Mr. Devereaux nodded slowly. Marilyn began the long practice of cleaning herself.

"And I take it the toy will never be yours?" Mr. Devereaux said.

Oscar felt ridiculous hearing it in those terms, hardly something that should be causing a twelve-year-old to despair.

"It's not even that special," Oscar lied.

"Ah, but the toy is only the stem that breaks ground," Mr. Devereaux said, and Oscar looked up from his feet to stare into the old man's eyes. He might have been slipping into one of his lapses.

But Oscar was surprised to see Mr. Devereaux looking right at him.

"The reason for the wanting is what lies underneath. It's the soil that feeds the want."

Mr. Devereaux leaned a little closer to Oscar, pressing his veiny arm against the guard rail enough to make Oscar nervous.

"I think you have tilled quite a lot of soil in your handful of years on this earth," he said. "So much wanting . . . but you've never been able to pluck the fruits of your labor from the ground, have you?"

Oscar was never any good at growing things. He killed every plant he tried to water, every fish he tried to nurture.

"I don't think you know—" he started, but Mr. Devereaux didn't let him finish.

"The best cultivators are the ones who know when the right time is to pick the crop," he said, and Oscar was trying, he really was, but Mr. Devereaux was losing him fast.

"Mr. D., you're real nice to try—"

"Ugh," Mr. Devereaux groaned like something hurt. He leaned away from his position against the rail and arched his back. Oscar could hear something pop deep inside the man's rickety bones. Marilyn paused her bath long enough to make sure Mr. Devereaux was okay.

"A *grower*, maybe, but a *thinker* you're not," Mr. Devereaux said to Oscar. "Sometimes you have to know when to go for it, even when it doesn't look possible."

Oscar stared at Mr. Devereaux.

"Quit sitting here and go find your precious toy!" Mr. Devereaux yelled, his phlegmy throat catching on the words, and he began to hack. Marilyn wound herself into a tight ball on her chair.

The new orderly appeared out of nowhere, standing in the doorway but reluctant to walk any closer.

"Is everything all right in here, Mr. Dev—?"

"No, everything is not all right, you daft ferret! Go and get me a glass of water, for the love of . . ."

The orderly scurried away, but Oscar couldn't seem to get up from his chair. He was frozen in place, contemplating the prophecy he'd received in a haze of cat hair and disinfectant.

"What? You don't think she looks like a ferret? No one should have a face that small," Mr. Devereaux said to Oscar.

"But what if it's sold out everywhere?" Oscar said, his brain finally coming back online.

"Don't you young people have the Internet? Or your computer phones or i-whatzits? Somebody has the stupid toy somewhere," said Mr. Devereaux, coughing up a little more phlegm. "The point is, quit tilling. It's time to pick."

The orderly returned with a small yellow cup, and Mr. Devereaux took it from her roughly before turning on his side, his back to her and to Oscar. Marilyn poked an ear up to be sure all was well before resettling into her coil.

In the space of five seconds, Mr. Devereaux was snoring loudly, his ribs rising and falling inside his threadbare pajamas.

"Looks like you tuckered him out," the orderly said to Oscar as they shuffled out the door, closing it behind them. "You're my hero."

Oscar felt dizzy by the time he made his way back to the front desk. His mom was hustling down the hall with three orderlies in tow, each following her like ducklings struggling to keep up.

"You're a good soul," his mom said to Oscar without looking up from her clipboard. Oscar knew she meant it, though. She was just busy.

"He calls the new orderly a ferret," Oscar said.

His mom shrugged and mumbled something about a small face.

"Anyway, I told Raj and Isaac I'd meet up with them,"

Oscar said, slinging his backpack over his shoulder.

"Oh? Anything fun happening?" she asked, still absorbed in her paperwork. One of the orderlies was trying to get her attention.

Oscar stared at the top of his mom's head, the gray streak that ran from her cowlick to her crown suddenly looking larger, like age had poured over her head while she slept one night.

"Nah," he said. "Nothing special."

She cupped his chin gently in her palm, finally looking up, and Oscar smiled back because she was always trying her hardest. She always had.

He turned on his heel toward the doors.

"Oh, Oscar, can you pick up some yog—?"

"Sorry, Mom! Gotta run!" Oscar said as he fled the lobby and returned to the safety of the vestibule. He was almost out the door when Irvin, still bobbing his head to whatever played in his ears, yelled over the music.

"You got a message!" he said.

"Huh?" said Oscar.

"What?" said Irvin, then pulled his headphones around his neck. "You got a message. From the short one, what's his name? Isaac."

"He called here for me?" Oscar said, utterly confused. He couldn't remember a single time his friends had ever tried reaching him here, even though it seemed like he spent just as much time at Royal Oaks as he did in his own home. If anything, sometimes Raj or Isaac would wait for Oscar to finish helping his mom, wasting time in the vestibule while Irvin ignored them.

"Said you gotta meet them at the mall. Something about a trap," Irvin said.

"The mall? Not the Toy Box? Wait, when did they call??" Oscar demanded, which got Irvin's attention.

"Well, let me just check the messaging service," he said, reaching for an imaginary memo pad.

"Sorry, it's just—"

"Ten minutes maybe," Irvin said, softening.

Ten minutes. If it took him twenty on the bus, another ten to walk from the bus stop to the mall, there might still be time to get there before they close.

"I gotta go!"

"Have fun . . . meh, whatever," Irvin said as he pulled his headphones back over his ears, the doors already swishing closed behind Oscar.

Oscar danced around the bus stop like he had to pee, leaning off the sidewalk into the street to see if he could spot the marquee on every passing bus. Drivers honked him out of the way, but he barely noticed them.

Finally, the number 56 bus arrived, slowing to an agonizingly long stop and sighing down to meet the curb. It was standing room only, and Oscar felt irrational fury toward anyone who dared to pull the stop cord. It seemed there wasn't a two-block stretch where they didn't stop to let someone on or off, and Oscar was about to burst with impatience.

When the mall stop finally came, he was so eager to get off, he nearly forgot to pull the cord for himself.

"Whoa whoa, here!" he yelled up to the driver, who grumbled something about not being his personal chauffer. Oscar hollered a quick apology over his shoulder as he booked it through the thick grove of eucalyptus trees that were definitely someone's private property to get to the mall's east entrance, the closest one to the Emporium.

The Emporium had nearly closed three different times, always on the verge of bankruptcy, always rescued at the last minute by some mystery financier who, according to chipper new anchors on the evening broadcast, couldn't bear to see another independent business succumb to one of the big chain toy stores. It might have been an act of charity if the Emporium hadn't been so gross.

Oscar was pretty sure the place had never been mopped. Mystery splatters lined the baseboards all around the cavernous store, not a single stain ever moving from where it had made its home. Oscar himself had made one of those stains when he was eleven, puking up an entire Radiation Green Big Slurp right in front of the beach ball display. Though he tried not to look, every time he went into the Emporium, he saw the telltale green flecks that had never been thoroughly scrubbed from the back wall.

The store seemed to always be half lit, the fluorescent

lights high above buzzing and flickering like they resented being on. But maybe the most depressing part of the Emporium was its perpetually unstocked shelves. They'd carry maybe a handful of the really good toys everyone was clamoring for that year, but the rest of the cavernous store was occupied by half-emptied displays of dusty generic dolls, action figures, and play sets that the parents who were too late or too broke had to resort to. Oscar knew for a fact his mom had stopped into the Emporium more than a few times, always at the end of her nightly shift, looking for the closest facsimile to a brand-name toy her small paycheck could buy. Oscar never let her see his disappointment.

But the Emporium was the only toy shop located in the mall; all the rest in town were the big stand-alone stores. If Isaac was telling him to meet them there, they must know something that everyone else in the entire town didn't.

Only that didn't seem to be the case once Oscar opened the door to the east entrance. Even from far away, he could see a squirming line of people trying to squeeze into the Emporium. It was more foot traffic than the store probably saw in a year.

Oscar slowed to a walk as he approached the crowd with caution, so unnerved by the sight of that many people pushing to get into the Emporium of all places.

Sure enough, there at the register by the door, a single petrified teenager was failing spectacularly at urging people to be patient. Poor guy probably had zero idea of what he was walking into that day for his shift.

"Oscar!"

Oscar searched for Isaac in the crowd, but as Irvin had reminded him less than an hour before, Isaac was the short one. He was hard enough to find in a crowd half this size.

"Over here!"

That time, it was Raj, and finally, after sweeping the jostling crowd three times, Oscar spotted his friend jumping above the surrounding heads. He wasn't all that far from the front of the line, which had to mean they somehow got the inside track on the inventory.

Oscar squeezed his way past a gaggle of angry customers.

"Hey, there's a system here, kid," one guy growled, and Oscar had to hide his laugh because . . . *really*? This was a system?

Oscar ducked a couple more grumbles before finally reaching Raj and Isaac, the latter on tiptoe trying to see how far they were to the front.

"Dude, we tried the Toy Box, Marbles, and that place on Twenty-Third and San Juan," said Raj, skipping right to the point.

"We even went to that weird organic place on Fifth Street that only sells wooden toys," said Isaac.

"If they ever had it at all, they sold out in like five minutes," said Raj.

"But the Emporium has them?" Oscar asked, still in disbelief. He hadn't actually *seen* anyone leave with one, and seeing was believing.

"Not on the shelves," Raj said, getting to the good part. "We saw Thad outside of Rockets, and he was holding this big Emporium bag, so we knew something had to be up. He didn't want to, but he showed us."

"Well, he showed us the top of the box, but he definitely had one. He was all smug about it," said Isaac. "I guess his sister's dating the assistant manager here, and he said they got a small stock of 'em, but the manager wasn't putting them on the shelf."

"Probably wanted to sell them himself online," Raj said. "Jerk."

"Guess word got out," Oscar said, watching the crowd watch everyone else. No one wanted to be the first in line to hear "We just sold the last one."

The crowd surged suddenly, knocking the entire quasi-line forward, and a general rumble of protest burbled from the customers.

Isaac fell against Oscar, who fell against the lady in front of him, who complained louder than the rest.

"*Excuse* me," she said, only half turning to shoot Oscar a dirty look.

The secretary. Ms. Beastly. The one with five nephews.

"Oh no," Oscar whispered. "She's gonna clean them out!" he hissed to Raj and Isaac.

"She can't. Limit's one per customer," said Raj. "Don't worry, I've got a good feeling."

"Oh well, if you have a feeling," Oscar rolled his eyes, but secretly he was grateful for Raj's optimism. It's not like Oscar had any of his own to offer. Mr. Devereaux's pep talk about harvesting was a distant memory.

After an entire eon had passed, the line crawled forward, and the secretary from the boys' school was next.

"What do you mean limit one per person?"

"Sorry, ma'am, that's the rule," said the clerk, looking like he was maybe seconds from a meltdown.

"Whose rule?"

"My manager's, ma'am," he said, and the line behind them sighed loudly.

"Haven't you been listening, lady? He's said it a hundred times already," groaned one guy unlucky enough to still be squeezed against the shelf closest to the door.

"Well, what am I supposed to tell my nephews?" Ms. Beastly asked, matching the guy's grumpiness.

"How about you tell them, oh, I don't know, that the limit was one per person!" the guy said, and Oscar had to admire his spunk. No one at school dared to talk to the secretary that way.

"Ma'am," the clerk interrupted, "I can sell you one, but you'll have to move along."

The secretary gave him a look that Oscar was pretty sure could melt human brains.

"I mean, uh, if it's okay?" he said, but it was too late. He was already liquefying.

Ms. Beastly slammed her giant purse on the counter and huffed her way through counting out her cash, then exchanged it for one glorious Plushtrap Chaser.

It was the first time Oscar had actually seen one in the flesh . . . or stuffing, or whatever.

Even from behind the cellophane window of the box, the thing looked perfectly terrifying. Its plastic eyes bulged from even wider eye sockets, making the face look skeletal. The mouth hung open to reveal lines of unsettlingly pointed canine-looking teeth. With the toy standing almost three feet tall, the clerk had to stand on tiptoe to get the box over the counter and into the secretary's grasping hands, and she shooed away the plastic bag he offered, decidedly done with this entire transaction. She walked away in a huff, dozens of eyes following her purchase out the door before returning their attention to the keeper of the treasure.

The crowd surged forward, but it wasn't necessary. Oscar, Raj, and Isaac were practically crawling over the counter.

"One Plushtrap Chaser, please!" Oscar said breathlessly. "If there's only one left, we can split it." The boys shoved their hands into their pockets to pool their money, a compromise they hadn't even needed to discuss. If one Plushtrap was all they could get, then they'd just have to share it—all for one and all that. They understood how scarcity worked.

"Sorry," the guy behind the counter said, but he didn't look sorry so much as terrified.

"What do you mean 'sorry'?" Oscar said, but on some level he already knew.

"No . . . nononononono," Isaac shook his head. "Don't say it."

The clerk swallowed, his Adam's apple traveling up and down his neck.

"We're . . . sold out."

The crowd erupted in protest, and whether it was conscious or not, the clerk gripped the counter like he expected the floor to fall out from under him.

"It can't be," Raj said, but Oscar could barely hear him over the roar of angry customers. He looked at Oscar like he was begging him to lie and tell him it was all just a joke. There was enough for them. They wouldn't walk away empty-handed.

It couldn't possibly be that Oscar had come so far for another *almost*.

But Oscar looked at the petrified face of the clerk. What reason would he have for lying now? More than that, what reason would he have for angering a crowd already on the brink of revolt?

The seed of disappointment was sprouting its roots in Oscar's stomach as the scene before him played out in slow motion. He pictured himself walking away with Raj and Isaac, circling the mall and dragging their feet back to the bus stop, unable to find the words to express this particular brand of letdown. Unable to describe how it wasn't the Plushtrap Chaser, not really. It was the confirmation that people like him weren't meant to hope for things.

While the clerk stood with his hands up, like his trembling palms could somehow comfort the angry masses, Oscar drifted to the side of the counter and tried to process yet another disappointment. He felt cut off from the scene around him . . . until a few intriguing words lured his attention away from the crowd's raucous protests and the clerk's weak responses.

". . . call . . . police," a woman's voice said.

"Who . . . processed . . . return?" a gruff man's voice demanded.

". . . real," a squeaky teenager's voice said.

". . . human?" the woman asked.

Oscar inched past the counter and peered around a few stacks of cardboard boxes. Just beyond the boxes, three employees clustered around something Oscar couldn't see.

Though their backs were mostly to Oscar, he was far enough from the crowd now that he could hear the employees discussing whatever it was they were looking at.

"No doubt about it. They look . . . real," said a teenaged staffer as he hunched over the thing.

"They're sure not from the manufacturer," said a man gruffly, who Oscar guessed to be the greedy manager, judging by his authoritative tone.

"How do you know?" asked a third employee, her low ponytail slung over her shoulder as she knelt beside the teenagers. "Did anyone look at this one before it was sold?"

"Someone would have noticed, wouldn't they?" the teenager asked.

"I still think we should call the police," the woman in the ponytail said, her voice lowering so that Oscar had to strain to hear her.

"And say what?" said the teenager. " 'Hey, we think we've got a situation here. See, someone returned a toy and, funny story, now the toy looks too lifelike! Help, officer, help!' "

"Keep your voice down!" scolded the maybe-manager.

"I mean, they can't *actually* be real, can they?" the woman asked.

The other two said nothing, and as though on cue, all three stepped away from the thing they were crowding around, and Oscar could finally see what they were examining.

There, on top of a small worktable, sat a mangled box that looked like it had been rescued from a trash compactor. Its cellophane window was dingy, with white crease marks spread like veins across the front. The corners of the box were soft and worn, and the top flap was held together by a fuzzy strip of packing tape. But even through all this damage, Oscar could see a green head and bulging eyes.

A Plushtrap Chaser!

Beyond Oscar, the crowd's unhappiness crescendoed into

a roar, and the clerk suddenly appeared behind the boxes. He didn't notice Oscar. He was too panicked.

"Help!" the clerk shouted at the other employees. "They're about to revolt!"

Before they turned, Oscar slipped back around the boxes. No longer eavesdropping on the employees, he ran to his friends, who were still pressed against the counter.

The woman appeared beside the register and the panicked clerk. Her name tag said she was "Tonya, Assistant Manager."

"I'm very sorry," Tonya called out, "but the Plushtrap toy is now out of stock."

"No, it isn't," Oscar said, too quietly at first, and he was impossible to hear over the tumultuous crowd.

When Tonya didn't respond, he shouted, "Hey!"

She turned to him, her dark eyes intense. "What?" she snapped.

"You have one back there," Oscar said. Maybe he accused. He pointed to where he knew the Plushtrap Chaser was behind the stacks of boxes.

Tonya shot another look at the crowd, then glanced in the direction Oscar was pointing. She stared that way a little too long, then looked at Oscar like they were suddenly the only two people in the store.

"That one's damaged," she said.

"It looks fine to me," Oscar lied, pressing his luck. He wasn't sure what Tonya and the other employees had been talking about, but he was smart enough to know something weird happened to the returned Plushtrap Chaser. He didn't care, though. His need for the toy was all-consuming.

"It's not fine, kid. It's . . . um, defective," Tonya crossed her arms. "Trust me, you don't want that one."

"But—"

"It's not for sale!" Tonya said through gritted teeth before yelling into the crowd, "Folks, I'm sorry, okay? I'm sure we'll get some more at some point!"

Then she grumbled to himself, "We'd better."

"When will that be?" demanded a woman in a shirt that said KEEP CALM AND DANCE ON.

"I don't—"

"What am I supposed to tell my daughter?" a guy in a suit and tie asked.

"Sir, you must—"

"Your clerk said you had Plushtraps for everyone!" hollered a lady so close to Oscar, his ear rang with her shrill echo.

"I doubt he said—"

The crowd was on the verge of mutiny, but Oscar barely registered them.

"Dude, we'd better get out of here," Isaac said.

"No joke," said Raj. "My mom dragged me to some sale on bedsheets once. When they ran out, I actually saw this one lady bite someone. They were out for blood."

Isaac looked at Raj in horror. "I don't want to get bit."

But Oscar was still only half listening.

"I don't care if it's damaged. I'll buy it anyway," he said

to Tonya, but the crowd was too loud for her to hear him. She was unwinding the cord on the intercom.

"People, please calm down!" she yelled into the microphone as feedback pierced the air, making everyone pause for a moment to cover their ears. But that only seemed to rile them up more, and soon customers were shoving and flooding the store, tearing toys off the shelves as they looked for hidden Plushtrap Chasers like they were on some sort of demented Easter egg hunt.

"That's it. I'm calling security," Tonya yelled, then traded the microphone for the tan receiver under the cash register. "I don't get paid enough for this."

"C'mon, let us just buy the one you have back there," Oscar persisted. It was too much, the thought of leaving after coming this close. He couldn't bear it.

"Get lost, kid!" Tonya yelled over her shoulder before pressing the receiver to her ear. "Where's Mr. Stanley? Tell him I need some help over here," she said into the phone.

Then Tonya turned her back on the counter.

Oscar didn't think.

If he'd been thinking, he never would have run around the counter and behind the stacks of boxes. He never would have shoved aside the teenage employee and the maybe-manager who stood gaping at the crumpled three-foot box standing between them. He sure wouldn't have grabbed the box. He wouldn't have hoisted it up, accidentally clipping the teenaged staffer in the chin while the clerk and Tonya yelled for Oscar to stop, to wait, to put it down. If he'd been thinking, Oscar would have answered Raj and Isaac when they suddenly appeared beside him, asking him what the heck he was doing.

In that moment, the only thing bouncing around Oscar's head were Mr. Devereaux's words: *The point is, quit tilling. It's time to pick.*

Oscar slammed their pile of pooled cash on top of the worktable. He clutched the long, narrow box to his chest, turned, and ran around the counter. Then he dropped his shoulder to plow through the crowd that barely took notice of him, so invested they were in their own mayhem.

"Stop! STOP!" yelled the employees, but Oscar was already to the front door of the Emporium, which was suddenly clear now that the crowd had moved inside.

"Dude, what're you doing?!" called Raj, but he was nearly beside Oscar, so it was clear that whatever he was doing, he wasn't doing it alone. Oscar could hear Isaac's short legs working double-time to keep up behind them.

"That way!" the clerk yelled, still too close to Oscar to be comfortably far away. "They took it. They stole it!"

"Stop!" yelled another voice, and this one somehow sounded more authoritative.

"Oh man, it's security!" Isaac wheezed, and suddenly, he was faster than Oscar and Raj, sprinting ahead of them and leading the way out of the mall, the east entrance now in sight.

"We're dead," Raj said, but he was keeping pace with Oscar. "We're so incredibly dead."

Oscar couldn't say anything. He could hardly process what his body was doing. His mind had completely left the building.

Suddenly, Isaac swerved, and it only took Oscar a second to see why. Emerging from a restroom doorway to the right was a confused mall security guard hiking up his pants, watching the scene in front of him unfold with slow recognition of the problem.

Oscar and Raj sped past him just as the guard behind them yelled, "Stop them!"

The east entrance glowed ahead like a beacon of safety, and Isaac burst through the door first, holding it while swinging his arm to Oscar and Raj.

"Hurry up hurry up hurry up!"

Oscar and Raj raced through, and the boys ran like a speeding arrow, Isaac at the head, while they made a hard right toward the private eucalyptus grove, but the parking lot was a wide expanse of obstacles before the trees.

Isaac hesitated, and Oscar took the lead, weaving past minivans and SUVs like they were playing a human arcade game, the obstacles in security uniforms likely to come out of every corner.

Except it was still only the two voices Oscar could hear behind them, and when he ventured a brief look over his shoulder, it was indeed still just the two, and at least the one from the restroom doorway looked like he was starting to run out of steam.

"Get . . ." he huffed between strides, "Back . . . Here!"

"We're losing them, c'mon!" Oscar finally said, his voice sounding like someone else's. It was like he'd left his body entirely, and this thieving, criminal escape artist had taken him over. He wasn't Oscar. In this moment, he wasn't anyone he recognized.

"We're almost there," Raj gasped, and they all knew he meant the eucalyptus grove. The menthol air was upon them, and the strong smell coated the inside of Oscar's burning lungs.

"That's private property!" Oscar could hear the other security guard yell, but he sounded farther away now. It was almost like he was telling himself that, not Oscar, so he wouldn't have to chase the boys once they'd crossed the tree line.

Oscar threw the box over the fence and followed it, tumbling to the ground and rolling through the leaves that had begun to shed now that fall was here. Isaac tumbled over the fence next, followed by Raj, and they took one more collective look through the slats in the fencing to confirm what Oscar already knew—the security guards had abandoned their pursuit, with the larger one resting his hands on his knees while he bent, huffing and spitting.

The boys weren't done running, though. It was private property, and they shouldn't be there, either, but it was more than that. It was wrong. They knew everything about what they'd just done was wrong. Especially what Oscar had done. Instead of facing that, he tried to outrun it.

He ran all the way to his street, even as Raj and Isaac pleaded with him to slow down, that the danger was over, that he was being crazy. They pleaded angrily, in fact, and Oscar knew that maybe it was because he'd gotten them into this mess. *He'd* been the one to grab the Plushtrap Chaser. *He'd* been the one to run like a bear was chasing him. *He'd* been the one to make them decide to run with him or leave him to his own terrible decision and all of its consequences.

When they finally arrived at Oscar's house, lungs burning and necks sweating, their legs shaking hard enough to be useless, they collapsed on the floor of Oscar's small living room, splayed in a circle around the three-foot-long box that was damp with perspiration and decorated with stuck-on dead leaves.

"Technically, it wasn't stealing," Oscar said, first to regain his breath and possibly his wits.

"You're an idiot," Isaac said, and he meant it.

"I left our money on the counter," Oscar said, but he knew it was laughable, and Raj punctuated that fact by laughing mirthlessly.

"You're an idiot," Isaac said again, just to be sure it registered this time, and Oscar nodded.

"Yeah, I know."

This time they did all chuckle, not quite a laugh, and none of them meant it, but it was enough for Oscar to know that even though they hated what he did, they didn't hate him. And besides, now they had a Plushtrap Chaser, regardless of how they got it.

But now that he could catch his breath, Oscar had time to reflect on the hushed conversation he'd heard between the Emporium employees. What was it they'd said? Something about the parts looking too real? It was hard to see why that would be a problem. The more lifelike the better, right?

Still, the way they'd all backed away from the toy . . . something definitely wasn't right about it.

Raj and Isaac knelt next to him. They were staring at their illegally obtained Plushtrap Chaser.

Raj glanced up at Oscar. "Are we going to open it?"

Were they? They'd come this far. Was Oscar really going to let some disgruntled employees at the saddest toy store on earth keep him from the Plushtrap Chaser now? After he'd finally seized the day? After he'd finally plucked the fruits of all his labors?

"Dude, are we opening this thing or not?" asked Raj.

"Okay," Oscar said. "Let's see what this beast can do."

It took some doing to get the thing out of its box. The molded plastic case that should have formed a protective shell over the toy had been crushed along with the rest of the packaging, and was now almost one with the toy itself, the plastic wedged into every joint of the rabbit's arms and legs. The twist ties that secured it to the mold had bent to hard knots that needed to be carefully unwound. And between the smeared and tired marked lettering, the instructions were essentially illegible.

Once the boys had finally freed it from its packaging, Oscar stood the Plushtrap Chaser on its oversize feet and straightened the joints at the knees to stabilize it. The toy was relatively light considering the machinery that had to be behind it. The heaviest parts of the rabbit were its weighted feet (presumably for ease of movement and balance) and head (presumably for ease of chomping).

"I don't know why, but it's not exactly how I'd imagined it," Raj said. Oscar and Isaac were quiet, which meant silent—if reluctant—agreement.

They didn't mean it in a snobbish way, though. Oscar had received more than his share of lightly damaged or refurbished toys, the byproduct of having more wants than money. And though Raj and Isaac could afford more, they never held that over Oscar's head.

It was more like nothing could possibly live up to the hype that had preceded the release of this toy that—let's face it—didn't do much of anything. It ran . . . fast. And it chomped . . . fast. The simplicity, the plainness of its functionality, had appealed to Oscar, but more than that, the Plushtrap was *wanted*. It was what everyone would have that year. It was what only the unlucky, the consistently passed over, would have to go without. Oscar couldn't be that kid again. He just couldn't.

"Um, is it just me or do the teeth look wrong?" Isaac pointed at the straight, slightly yellow, *human-looking* teeth that were visible through Plushtrap's partly open mouth.

"No doubt about it. They look . . . real."

Oscar had to admit the teeth looked a little off, definitely not like the ones he'd seen in the ads or in the one he saw Ms. Beastly buy.

"Yeah, they're not pointed," Raj said. "Why aren't they pointed?"

Oscar didn't volunteer anything.

"They're not pointed, but they're creepy," Isaac said. "They look"—he swallowed—"human."

"Yeah," Raj said. "They do. Weird."

"And what's with the eyes?" Isaac said. He reached out and poked one of the cloudy green eyes. "Ew!" He whipped his hand back and flicked his finger. "It's squishy!"

There was no denying it. Whatever was wrong with this Plushtrap Chaser's teeth and eyes was definitely what the employees were discussing in the back of the store.

Still, Oscar thought, *there's no way the parts could be real.*

He'd seen the eyeball when Isaac touched it, though. There was the tiniest give, like if he'd pressed on a peeled grape. There was no tap from his fingernail like there should have been on hard plastic.

And then there were the teeth . . .

"That's why they were so freaked out," Oscar mumbled, and he only realized he'd said that last bit aloud when Raj and Isaac turned to stare at him.

This is my punishment, Oscar thought. *This is what I get for being an idiot and stealing this stupid toy.*

"Okay, so I've gotta tell you something I overheard in the store," Oscar said at the end of a long, pained sigh.

"How did you overhear anything in there?" Isaac said, focusing on the wrong question.

Oscar shook his head. "Near the back room. These employees . . . they were all standing around the box talking about how it'd been returned, and how they should call the cops because . . ."

"Because the eyes and the teeth are HUMAN!" Raj blurted, as though his wildest morbid imaginings had come true.

"Uh, yeah," said Oscar. "I guess when you say it out loud, it sounds a little ridiculous."

"Yeah, completely ridiculous," Raj said, eyeing the Plushtrap Chaser.

"Totally," Isaac said, scooting a couple inches from the toy.

"I mean . . . it's not like any one of us got a really good look at one close-up," reasoned Oscar. "They're probably all—"

"Nightmarish?" guessed Isaac.

Raj turned to Oscar. "You managed to steal us the only Plushtrap Chaser that looks like a half-human hybrid."

"I think its eyes are following me," said Isaac.

"Maybe if we see it in action, we'll feel better," Oscar said, trying to reboot everyone's enthusiasm.

Raj shrugged. "Why not?"

Isaac shrugged, too, but then he held up the marred instructions. "I think we're on our own."

"Let's see what those human teeth can do," Raj said.

Isaac shivered. "Stop calling them that."

Oscar tried pulling at the Plushtrap's chin, but the jaw wouldn't budge. The mouth was only open enough to glimpse the humanlike teeth, but it wouldn't open any farther.

"Maybe if you push from its nose," Raj said, gripping the top half of the rabbit's face while Oscar continued to pull on the jaw.

"Here, you need more leverage," Isaac said, taking the rabbit's whiskers in his fists and yanking.

"Dude, you're gonna rip its face off," Oscar said, and stopped pulling a little too fast, sending Raj and Isaac rocking back on their heels.

"We just need something to pry it open," he said, trotting to the kitchen to grab a butter knife from the drawer. When he returned, he jammed the flat end of the knife into the partially opened mouth. But when he pressed on the knife, the thin metal gave suddenly, and the tip of the knife broke off inside the rabbit's mouth. The pointed end seemed to be stuck in its weird teeth.

"Whoa," Raj said. "Tell me it didn't take a bite out of a knife."

Oscar looked at him, once again tiring of the struggle the toy was bringing. The payoff of his actions was becoming more elusive by the minute.

"It didn't bite the knife, Raj. I broke it."

"Maybe it just needs to be turned on before it'll open," Isaac said, and finally, one of them was thinking clearly.

Oscar and the boys parted the fur on the back of the rabbit, searching for a switch to indicate it was off. All they found was a line of Velcro closed over a battery compartment, complete with one rectangular 9-volt battery tucked into its place. Below the battery compartment was a pattern of small holes.

"Is that a speaker?" asked Isaac. "Hang on, it talks?"

"Nah," Raj dismissed. "Not in any of the ads." His brow crinkled. "What does a rabbit even sound like?"

"Gentlemen, *focus*. We're looking for the power switch. Check its feet," Oscar said, and sure enough, when they turned it over, a little black switch pointed to the "on" position.

"Okaaaaay," Isaac said, and he reached for the switch, flicking it off, then on, then off again.

"Maybe it needs another battery," Raj said, and that sounded like as good a reason as any.

Oscar returned to the kitchen and rummaged through the junk drawer, sifting past rubber bands and orange juice coupons until he came upon an opened package of 9-volt batteries, with one left in the box.

"Try this one," Oscar said, hustling back to the living room.

The boys plucked the existing battery from its place, scraping away the little bit of white crust that had corroded the inside. They placed the new battery in the compartment and closed the cover.

Raj slapped his hands together and rubbed. "This is it!"

Oscar picked the rabbit up and flipped the switch on, but the Plushtrap remained dormant, its mouth locked in a mostly closed position.

"Oh, come ON!" Isaac complained, the stress of the day clearly beginning to have an effect.

"Hang on, hang on," Oscar said, doing his best to calm the room. He was turning the box over and over in his hands, and there in bold letters inside a comic book–style *POW* burst was a critical detail:

WALKS IN THE DARK!

FREEZES IN THE LIGHT!

"Guys, it only works when the lights are off," Oscar said, and his heart filled with the tiniest bit of hope that all wasn't lost.

"Oh," Raj and Isaac said in unison, as though it made perfect sense. Of course. Somehow they'd all managed to forget this one crucial detail.

The boys got right to work, pulling drapes shut and flicking lights off, surrounding the bunny in as much dark-ness as possible. But enough daylight still leaked through the curtains to illuminate the disappointment on their faces. The Plushtrap Chaser would chase nothing.

"It's just not dark enough yet," Isaac said.

"It probably has to charge or something," Raj offered.

But when neither Isaac nor Raj lobbied to take the Plushtrap home for the night, the last of Oscar's hope evaporated, leaving his insides feeling dry and cracked. It was just like everything else. He'd had the nerve to think something good might come his way. He'd even done the one thing he swore to himself and to his mom and to anyone whose opinion ever mattered to him that he'd never do: he'd stolen. All for the tiny drop of what could have been a taste—just a *taste*—of good fortune.

Now he was left without one third of $79.99, without one Plushtrap Chaser, and maybe even on the verge of losing the two friends who'd stuck their necks out for him when his thirst had become too great.

Oscar's mom called that night.

"Anything exciting happen today?" she asked, the same question she always asked when she was at work and he was at home, feeding himself dinner and putting himself to bed while she worked the night shift and took care of the old people.

"Nothing at all," he said, just like he always did. Only this time, it hurt so much more to say it because something exciting *had* happened . . . and then it hadn't.

★　★　★

Oscar woke to the smell of coffee like he did most mornings. His mom practically lived on the stuff. How she got home at three in the morning and woke up at seven Oscar had never been able to figure out.

When he rolled out of bed, he was momentarily startled by the gooey-looking eyes swimming in the gaping hollows of a green furry face. They really did look human.

"Whoa, hey there, creeper," he said to the Plushtrap. The rabbit stood at attention by his bedside, right where he left it last night, the tiny shard of a butter knife tip still stuck between two of the visible incisors.

But just like yesterday, it did absolutely nothing. Not that it should, given the daylight streaming in through the thin curtains behind Oscar's bed. It was possible he'd gone to bed with the hope that a night in his dark room would charge whatever power source hadn't been triggered by the boys the day before. It was just another stupid hope, though.

Oscar shuffled down the hall in his flannel pants and kissed his mom on the cheek like he always did. If Raj or Isaac ever saw him do that, they'd never let him forget it, but Oscar knew what it meant to his mom, and he didn't mind it so much. After his dad died, Oscar took up the habit without his mom ever asking. When he was too short to reach her head, he'd kissed her elbow, then her shoulder. It was just a peck, hardly even a kiss given that Oscar tucked his lips into his mouth, but disappointing his mom wasn't really an option.

After Oscar poured himself a glass of juice and a bowl of sugar flakes, he munched away as usual until he finally looked up and noticed his mom hadn't said a word to him. She was looking down at the newspaper they still had delivered every morning because, as she put it, a subscription was cheaper than a smartphone plan. She hadn't looked up even for a second.

His stomach instinctively dropped.

"What's up?" he asked, his voice pitched a little higher than usual.

His mom slurped her coffee slowly before pulling her mug away from her mouth, her head still down.

"Seems there was some sort of incident at the mall yesterday afternoon."

Oscar didn't think it was possible for his stomach to sink any lower, but it found a new depth in a hurry.

"Oh yeah?" he said, shoving a mound of sugar flakes into his mouth and doing his best not to throw it right back up.

"Mmhhmm," his mom said. "Says here the Emporium had to call security and everything," she said, taking another sip of coffee.

"Oh wow," Oscar said, spooning more sugar flakes into his mouth even though he wasn't finished chewing the first spoonful.

"All over some stupid toy. Apparently, a couple of kids even made off with one during the commotion."

Then Oscar's mom did look up, fixing her dark-brown

eyes on Oscar's. People were always telling them how much they looked alike, with their smooth features and eyes like coal.

"Can you believe that?" she asked, and Oscar understood that she was asking exactly that . . . if he could believe it. Because if he knew anything about it—anything at all—it wouldn't be so hard to believe it was true.

"Irvin mentioned something about you boys heading to the mall yesterday," she said, giving Oscar so many chances not to lie. She'd opened every single door to the truth, inviting Oscar to walk through, to be honest. She was begging him not to disappoint her.

But it wasn't just Oscar's lie to protect anymore. Oscar had made sure of that when he dragged Raj and Isaac along with him. So, Oscar made a decision: he disappointed his mom to save his friends.

"Must've been after we got there," Oscar said. Then he shrugged. A period on the end of the lie.

Oscar's mom stared at him for so long, he thought maybe he could apologize without saying a word. He hoped his mom could hear it. Instead, she finally released his gaze and drained the last drop of coffee from her mug, folded the paper over itself, and threw it into the recycling bin without another word.

Oscar had never felt smaller. He spent the rest of the day at home, avoiding Raj's calls and pretending he didn't hear Isaac knocking at his door. He lay in bed instead, staring at the bulging eyes of the Plushtrap while it stared back at him.

"You're worse than useless," he said to it. Or maybe he said it to himself.

The next few days passed by Oscar in a blur, and finally, Isaac and Raj cornered him in the cafeteria.

"Look, if you're possessed, we'll understand, okay?" Isaac said. "Just blink twice if you need help."

"C'mon, man. If you're trapped in there, let us help you," Raj said, nodding with Isaac.

"I'm not possessed," Oscar said, but he couldn't make himself smile.

"Dude, if this is still about the Plushtrap thing," Isaac said, and Oscar thought that was a funny way of referring to a misdemeanor.

"It's not just that," Oscar said, and Raj and Isaac got quiet. Oscar figured they probably understood. They'd been friends long enough for them to notice that Oscar's shoes never had the right logo, that his backpack had to last two school years instead of one.

"First-generation technology is always bogus anyway," Raj said. "We'll save up for Gen Two. It'll give them a chance to work out all the bugs."

Isaac nodded, and Oscar actually did feel better. They didn't hate him. He was down a mom and a Plushtrap, but he was up two friends. Things were starting to even out. That's probably what made the thing he had to say next even harder.

"I've gotta take it back."

Isaac put his palm to his forehead, and Raj just closed his eyes. Clearly, they'd seen this coming.

"With those eyes and those teeth in it?" Raj said. "C'mon, dude, just let it go."

"I can't. My mom knows."

They both looked up. "How are you even alive?" asked Isaac.

"I mean, she didn't *say* she knows, but she knows," said Oscar.

"What good will it even do?" asked Raj. "It's busted. Our money's already gone. And do you really want to answer questions about those, um, 'upgrades'?"

Raj and Isaac looked around to make sure no one had heard.

Oscar understood. It was bad enough owning up to the theft. Raj was right; he absolutely did not want to answer any questions about the eerily human eyes and set of matching human teeth.

Which is still impossible, Oscar told himself, even though he hadn't mustered the courage to touch the eyes for himself and swore that last night, those same eyes had followed him across the room.

He shook off the memory.

"That isn't the point," Oscar said, and Raj and Isaac couldn't say anything because they knew it was true. It wasn't about the money or the toy. It was about the taking. And Oscar wasn't a taker. None of them were.

"You guys don't have to come," he said. "I was the one who did it."

But Raj and Isaac just sighed and looked at their shoes, and Oscar knew he wouldn't be walking to the mall himself by that afternoon. His friends would be there with him.

"You're an idiot," said Isaac.

"I know."

For some reason, the box felt heavier in Oscar's hands on the way back to the mall. Maybe it was because of all the money they'd sunk into it.

"What if we see those security guards again?" Isaac asked, and they stopped just outside the doors to the east entrance.

Raj shook his head. "What're they gonna do, arrest us for returning what we stole?"

"Good point," Isaac said, and they began the slow walk to the Emporium.

But when they arrived, the Emporium was gone.

"What?" Oscar whispered as he read and reread the big orange letters lighting the place above the glass doors that used to be yellow. Now they spelled HAL'S HALLOWEEN HALLWAY.

"Did we come in the wrong entrance?" Raj asked, but they all knew they hadn't.

Any doubts that remained were laid to rest the minute

they walked through the door. The same stained and grimy floor spread the length of the store, but now, instead of shelves lined with dusty toys and dark spaces, every sort of Halloween accoutrement spilled from the metal racks. There was an aisle for decorations and lights, another for party favors, two for candy, and what looked to be five or six aisles crammed with every sort of costume, from murderous slashers to sparkly princesses.

"Did we fall through a wormhole or something?" Isaac asked, scratching the back of his neck.

"Hey, guys, look," Raj chuckled, pulling a green Plushtrap Chaser costume from the rack and holding it against him.

"Dude, seriously?" Isaac said, yanking the costume from Raj's hands and replacing it.

Oscar made his way to the cashier's counter at the front of the store, the scene of humanity's meltdown not even a week ago.

"Where's the Emporium?" asked Oscar in a daze.

The girl behind the counter wore a pair of yellow antennae on long springs that bounced when she looked down from her perch at Oscar.

"The what?"

"The store that was here before," Oscar said.

"Oh yeah," she said without answering the question, nor apparently caring to.

"Where'd it go?" Oscar asked.

"Not a clue," the girl said, returning to the screen of her

phone. "I just filled out an application and *poof*," she said, waving her hand lazily. "Here I am."

"But I need to return this," said Oscar, suddenly feeling very young and small next to this older girl.

The girl looked back down at him, and her eyes widened just enough to know he'd finally gotten her attention. It lasted only a second, though.

"Is that what I think it is?" she asked, looking at her screen again. "Why would you want to return it? You could sell that thing for a fortune."

"It's . . . it's not mine," Oscar said, looking down. When he looked back up, the girl had lifted the eyebrow closest to him.

"It is now."

Oscar looked back down at the box in his hands, the cardboard looking more crinkled than ever.

When he rejoined Raj and Isaac, they were decked out fully in hockey masks and pixie wings.

"I'm going for a kind of murderous fairy vibe," said Raj.

"I can't return it," Oscar said, and Isaac and Raj lifted their masks.

"Well . . . no one can say we didn't try, right?" Raj said.

"Maybe it's for the best," said Isaac, but he didn't follow it up with anything, so Oscar knew he couldn't think of a reason why.

★   ★   ★

Ten minutes and three sets of pixie wings and hockey masks later, the boys headed back to Oscar's house to devise a plan for trick-or-treating. Every year, they vowed to make it to the other side of the train tracks, where the good candy was rumored to be. Every year, they ran out of time, distracted by the false promise of the good stuff closer by.

"We fall for it every time," Raj said. "Not this year. This year, we start on the other side of the tracks and work our way back."

Oscar and Isaac agreed. It was a good plan.

The plan set, Raj and Isaac fell deep into a match to the death on Raj's newest console game, taking turns after wiping palm sweat from the controls before each turn.

"You're going down," Raj said, but his thumbs jammed furiously at the buttons while Isaac sat back smiling.

"Every time," Isaac said. "You say it every time. One day, you're just going to have to admit—"

"You're not the champion," Raj said, beads of sweat forming on his brow.

Oscar was barely paying attention, though. He was chiseling away the remaining battery leakage from the compartment on the back of the Plushtrap Chaser.

The wind was picking up outside, and it looked like the storm the news had been blathering on about for the last week was finally going to hit. The electricity kept flickering on and off, which was only contributing more to Raj's losing streak.

"C'mon, it doesn't count if the power goes out," Raj complained.

"I don't make the rules," Isaac said, smug in his luck.

It had to make Raj even angrier that the game was his; so was the console. He should be better at it, except that they mostly kept it plugged in at Oscar's because he was the only one without siblings hanging around begging to play. Oscar wasn't interested in video games right then, though.

"Oscar, help me out here. Power outages warrant a redo, don't they?" Raj asked while they waited for the power to come back on. The light outside was fading fast.

"Hmmm?" Oscar asked. He'd tried scraping away the rest of the gunk, swapping out the battery for one in the little fan that sat on his mom's bedside table, even turning the battery around to face the opposite charge, hoping maybe it was a manufacturing defect. Nothing powered the Plush-trap Chaser, though.

"Why are you still messing with that?" Isaac asked, clearly tired of the drama it had brought to the last several days.

"He's right," Raj said in a rare moment of agreement. "It's hopeless, Oscar. Just let it go."

"I think we should literally *let it go*," Isaac said, "as in get rid of it." He twisted his mouth for a second. "It's not just broken, it's . . . I don't know. Just wrong."

Oscar didn't disagree, but he wasn't going to admit it. He ignored Isaac, and he ignored Raj, too. But Oscar didn't feel like it was hopeless. They'd gotten away from mall security.

He'd kept the truth from his mom. They'd tried to do the right thing and return it. It was like there was some reason he had to keep this thing.

He flipped it over and stared into the murky glistening green eyes of the ugly rabbit.

"If you're possessed, blink twice," he said to the bunny, chuckling quietly.

Yet while the Plushtrap didn't blink, it emitted a sound. A sort of quiet chirp, so fast it might not have happened at all.

"Did you guys hear that?"

"Hear what?" asked Raj.

The power flickered back on, and the video game resumed, along with Raj and Isaac's arguing as they continued their tournament to the death.

Then, just as Oscar was getting ready to flip the rabbit over again and take his thousandth look at the battery compartment, he spotted a tiny hole at the side of the rabbit's metal jaw. At first, it looked like nothing but a bolt holding together the hinge of the lower jaw. From this angle, though, Oscar could see that it wasn't a bolt at all.

It was a port.

Oscar's house phone began to ring as the lights flickered again.

With the Plushtrap still in his hands, Oscar ran to the kitchen to catch the call before the machine picked up. Even if they could afford two phone plans, Oscar's mom would have insisted on keeping a land line. She was big on backup systems.

The line was crackly, and it took Oscar asking three times who it was before he could clearly hear his mom's voice.

"Ugh, this storm," his mom said. "How about now?"

"Yeah, I can hear you," Oscar said, barely listening. He was trying to get a closer look at the port on the Plushtrap, but it was hard when the light in the kitchen kept blinking out.

"LM, I need your help tomorrow," she said.

"Sure, Mom," he said, not listening.

"I'm sorry to ask. You know how much I hate asking. It's just that with this storm tonight, we've had so many people call in sick, we're going to be completely backed up on laundry and charts tomorrow, and . . . are you listening?"

"Uh-huh," Oscar lied, but it suddenly dawned on him why she sounded so apologetic.

"Wait, no, Mom. No, not tomorrow."

"I knew you'd be upset, hon, but it's—"

"Mom, tomorrow is Halloween!" Oscar said, suddenly panicked at what he'd agreed to, not that he'd have had much of a say in the matter either way.

"I realize that, but sweetie, aren't you and your friends a little old to be—?"

"No! Why do you always do that?" Oscar said, taking it a little too far, but now it was too late.

"Do what?"

Oscar could barely hear his mom now. The storm was

encroaching on the phone lines and rattling the house from the outside.

Maybe it was the fact that she sounded so far away that made Oscar feel like he could say what he said next.

"You act like I'm older, like I should be just like you. Like I should be just like Dad. You never let me be a kid. Dad died, and you expected me to just grow up."

"Oscar, I—"

"I stole it okay? I stole the stupid Plushtrap toy. Your Little Man *stole it!*" Oscar said, and he knew it was cruel, but he was just so angry because it was happening again. Once again, he was missing out on what everyone else got to enjoy.

The lights blinked off and on in the kitchen, and suddenly, his mom was gone.

"Mom?"

But all that greeted him was silence, then the echo of his own breath, and finally, the rapid tone of the circuit's busy signal.

Oscar walked slowly back to his room, just in time to watch Isaac put the finishing moves on Raj's fighter. All Oscar could do, though, was stare at the tiny port by the Plushtrap's jaw. The damage of what he might have just done to his mother was too much to contemplate all at once.

"Raj, I need your cell phone charger," Oscar said.

"What? Right now? I was just catching up!" he said, pointing to the screen.

"No, you weren't," Oscar said.

"Listen to the man," Isaac said. "He speaks the truth."

Oscar flinched at the reference to him as a 'man' and followed Raj to the hallway, where he fished a knotted cord from a drawer and handed it to Oscar.

Oscar knew it was a kindness of Raj not to ask what he'd need a phone charger for if he didn't have a phone, but Raj was still following Oscar's motions with interest.

Back in Oscar's room, Isaac had Raj's fighter's HP down to ten percent.

Oscar took a small breath and held it, then brought the charger's A-connecter to the hole in the Plushtrap's head. When the plug fit snugly in place, Oscar exhaled.

"This is it, Raj. I'm putting you out of your misery in three . . . ,"

The sound of Isaac's fighter powering up for his death move pulsed in Oscar's ears as he marched the Plushtrap and charger to the outlet across the room.

"Two . . ." said Isaac as the lights began to flicker overhead.

"Just get it over with," Raj said miserably.

"And you're de—"

Oscar didn't remember plugging the adapter into the wall. He didn't remember the lights going out, or Isaac's fighter winning the golden belt. If he was pressed, he might not be able to remember his own name.

All he knew for the moment was that the room was dark, and he was on the other side of it.

"What the . . . ?" he could hear Isaac say.

"Do you smell burning?" he could hear Raj say.

"Oh—oh man, Oscar," Isaac said.

"Oscar? Oscar!" said Raj.

Oscar couldn't understand why they seemed so panicked. He could barely make out the outline of their heads in the moonlight that illuminated the room in flicks and whips while the tree branches outside waved under the storm.

"Oscar, how many fingers am I holding up?" said Raj.

"You're not holding anything up," Isaac said, and Raj shook his head.

"Right. Sorry."

"I'm fine," Oscar said, not certain that was true, but he was getting weirded out with them acting so worried about him. "What's wrong with you guys?"

"Uh, do you not remember soaring across the room?" Raj said, and they looked even more worried now.

"Knock it off," Oscar dismissed, using the wall for support as he struggled to get to his feet. His head felt like it was stuck in a fish tank.

"We're not messing with you," Isaac said, and a closer look at their faces told Oscar it was true.

"One minute, you're plugging in the charger, the next minute, you're airborne. I think it was the lightning."

Outside, the moon fought for space in the sky against the invading clouds. Inside, Oscar's vision blurred for a moment longer until he finally felt things come into focus.

"Maybe we should call his mom," he heard Isaac say.

"No! No, don't call her," Oscar said, and they both looked worried again.

"What if your brain shorted out or something?" Raj said.

"I'd still be smarter than you," Oscar murmured.

"He's fine," said Isaac.

Oscar tried the light switch by the door. "Dead."

Isaac tried the remote for the television, but the screen stayed dark. "Nothing."

"Well, I guess that settles it," Raj said, heading for the living room where their sleeping bags were. "We have no choice but to get sick on Scorching Hot Cheese Knobs and knock out tomorrow night's plan."

Raj and Isaac headed for the living room, but Oscar lagged behind in his room. Halloween—for a precious minute, he'd forgotten that he wouldn't be able to go trick-or-treating. As the clouds swept away from the moon, Oscar looked across the room and saw the blackened scorch line beginning at the outlet and traveling up the wall.

"Great," Oscar muttered. "Something else to apologize for."

He was already formulating his explanation to his mom when he swore he saw a flicker of movement from the Plushtrap Chaser, still miraculously plugged into the fried outlet.

"Was that you?" he said, but the ugly green rabbit merely stared back at him, the glow of moonlight making its buggy eyes seem to shimmer. Oscar closed his bedroom door so he wouldn't have to look at his series of mistakes.

Just as the door clicked shut, Oscar swore, beyond all reason, that he heard Raj's voice from the other side of the door.

"Lights out," it said, with the faintest trickle of a giggle on the end of the sentence.

Oscar flung the door open, his eyes moving straight to the Plushtrap.

"What did you say?"

"Huh?" asked Isaac, already down the hall on his way to the living room.

"You heard that, right?"

"Heard what?"

Oscar turned back to his room. "C'mon, Raj, it's not funny."

"What's not funny?" Raj asked, poking his head around the corner at the other end of the hall.

Oscar shook his head. "Nothing. Never mind."

"Are you sure you're okay?" said Isaac, and Oscar conjured another laugh.

"Stupid storm's making me hear things."

In the living room, Raj and Isaac had torn into two bags of chips and were slurping Electric Blue Fruit Punch at a record pace.

Isaac belched. "Okay, so if we start here, just over the train tracks, we can work our way south," he said.

They were studying Raj's glowing phone, opened to a map of the town that centered on the split by the rail line between the east and west side. It wasn't lost on Oscar that they lived on the wrong side of the tracks, a joke that was a little too on-the-nose to make even with his friends.

"No, we need to start south and work our way north," said Raj.

"But we'll waste all our time in transit," argued Isaac, punctuating his point with another loud burp.

"Dude, I could smell that one," said Raj, scooting away. "And we'll move faster between houses if we're not already weighted down by candy. It's all about aerodynamics," he said.

Oscar had been watching the plan hatch from the kitchen while he quietly crumbled. The boys finally noticed him standing there.

"Fine, Oscar can break the tie," Raj said. "Where do we start, Oscar? North or south end of the tracks?"

"I can't go."

Raj let his phone drop to the floor. He and Isaac exchanged a look, and Oscar tried hard not to believe they hadn't seen this coming. But Oscar was forever having to skip out on plans when his mom called on him. Her Little Man.

"It's my mom," he said unnecessarily. "She needs . . ." He couldn't even bring himself to finish.

"Eh," Isaac said, putting on his best act. "It'll be lame anyway."

Raj played along as usual. "I bet the full-size candy bars are just a myth."

Isaac nodded. "And we'll split the stash three ways."

Oscar knew they were lying about it being epic. He knew they'd divvy their haul with him. He knew they were disappointed. But he'd never felt more grateful for his friends.

"Whoa, is that a white streak in your hair?" Isaac said, pointing at Oscar's head, pivoting the conversation.

Oscar reached for his head. "Seriously?"

Isaac chuckled. "No, but I'm sure you fried a few brain cells back there."

Raj cackled. "Not that you could afford to lose any."

For the first time that night, Oscar felt settled. Maybe everything would be okay. He didn't have a Plushtrap Chaser or a cell phone or Halloween. He didn't have his dad. But he had a mom who needed him, and he had friends who had his back.

Oscar had just taken his place beside Raj and Isaac on the living room floor when a spear of lightning tore through the sky. The light was so bright, at first Oscar thought his vision had blinked out. But when the light didn't return, and only the shadows and shapes of his living room surrounded him, he realized the rest of the house's power must have gone out.

"Uh, I think maybe you did a little more damage than just shorting out the socket," Raj said through the dark.

Oscar stood and felt his way to the window, which was harder to see than before because whatever moonlight that had made it through the storm earlier was gone now, covered by a thick layer of thunderheads.

"Nah," he said, pressing his cheek to the glass. "The power's out everywhere. Lightning must have hit the grid."

Isaac snorted. "Bet it's not out on the east side. Ever wonder how theirs never seems to get hit?"

"Hang on, I'll get some flashlights," Oscar said. "Mom bought a second one after the last time the power went out."

"That one lasted almost two days," Raj remembered. "We had to throw away half the food in our fridge."

"Two days with no TV, no games," Isaac said, shivering.

"My phone lost charge by the middle of the first day," said Raj. The boys stared into their memories of the Great Power Outage of May before shaking off the horror.

Oscar handed Isaac the cheap, lightweight flashlight and kept the heavier one for himself.

"Gonna have to use your phone flashlight," Oscar said to Raj. "We only have two."

"Sure, go ahead. Run my battery down," Raj pouted.

Suddenly, the boys heard a *thump* coming from the other end of the house.

Oscar might have been able to dismiss it as his imagination if Isaac and Raj hadn't reacted, too.

"Did you get a cat or something?" asked Isaac.

Oscar shook his head, then remembered they couldn't see him. He flicked on his flashlight, and Isaac followed suit.

Another *thump* echoed from the same place, and Oscar swallowed audibly.

"Maybe a tree branch against the window," Raj offered, but he didn't sound convinced.

Isaac shook his head and charged forward. "This is stupid."

"Hang on—" Oscar said, but Isaac was already halfway down the hall.

When they rounded the corner, another thump, this one decidedly louder, greeted them from behind Oscar's closed bedroom door. The house was too dark to detect any sort of shadow from the crack under the door, but the source of the sound was unmistakable. Something was banging slowly against the door in Oscar's room.

"So it was a 'no' on the cat then," whispered Isaac, his voice shaking.

"It's not a cat," Oscar hissed, and Raj shushed them.

As though in response to their voices, the banging stopped, and the boys held one collective breath.

Then, all at once, the banging started again, this time twice as fast, and with so much force it shook the door.

The boys slowly backed away but didn't dare take their eyes off the door.

"Still think it's a tree branch?" Isaac shot at Raj.

"Not unless the tree climbed into my room," said Oscar.

"You guys, shut up!" said Raj, holding up his hand. "Do you hear that?"

"What is that?" Oscar whispered.

"It sounds like . . . scraping," said Isaac.

They didn't have to wait long to find out. There, underneath the doorknob, a jagged hole in the plywood began to emerge, dug by a row of persistent, human-looking teeth strong enough to bite through a butter knife. As they dug, the teeth seemed to change shape, sharpening as they worked.

"No way," Oscar breathed.

"I thought it was broken!" yelled Raj, almost accusingly.

"It was!" said Oscar.

"Can we please argue about this somewhere else?" said Isaac, watching the quick progress the sawlike teeth were making on the area around the doorknob.

"Dude, it's a toy," said Raj. "What do you think it's gonna—?"

Then, with two more powerful bangs against the door, the bronze knob fell from Oscar's bedroom door, and it swung open to reveal a three-foot shadow with long, crooked ears. And while the Plushtrap was a mere shadow, its gleaming jagged teeth shone even in the dark.

And was that blood around the edges of the front teeth? How was that possible? Unless the teeth were human and the gums were human, too, but then, would they still bleed? It was all impossible . . . so impossible he couldn't bring himself to say any of it out loud.

Then, all at once, the Plushtrap Chaser ran straight for Oscar, Raj, and Isaac.

"go, go, GO!" Raj screamed, and they sprinted down the hallway. Oscar heard a small clunk and nearly tripped over whatever it was.

"In here!"

The boys darted to the next closest room—Oscar's mom's—and slammed the door behind them. Raj shoved the others aside to lock it.

"Really? You think it can turn knobs?" said Isaac, trying to catch his breath.

"I don't know what the heck it can do!" yelled Raj.

Then the banging began, this time on the door closest to them, and the boys stepped away in unison, watching the door bow under the force of a three-foot bunny.

Oscar's eyes widened as he heard the telltale sounds of scraping. The Plushtrap was about to chew through this door, too.

"How do we stop this thing?" said Isaac. "The switch is under its foot, right?"

They continued to back away as the scraping grew faster, the rabbit's skills appearing to improve with practice.

Oscar looked around the room frantically.

"Well, we'd better think of something quick, or that

thing's gonna eat through this door, too, and I don't think we can all fit in the bathroom," said Raj.

"Uh . . . uh . . ." Oscar was beginning to grow frantic as the chewing sped up.

"Oscar," Isaac said, and Isaac shined his flashlight at the hole beginning to form by the doorknob.

"Quick, climb up on something. The highest thing you can!" said Oscar, and they each found a surface: Oscar on the vanity, Isaac on the dresser, and Raj perched precariously on top of the headboard.

In no time, the rabbit had chewed through this door, too, and with a loud *thunk*, the doorknob fell to the carpet. Slowly, the door creaked open to once again reveal the vacant stare and crooked ears of the green rabbit.

The boys held their breath and waited to see what the Plushtrap would do. It took very little time for the bunny to make up its mind. A machine bent on its one job, it headed straight for the object in front of it, the dresser, and began to drag its jagged teeth across the wood of the wardrobe's legs.

"Are you kidding me?" screamed Isaac, watching in horror as the bunny made fast work of one of the dresser's ornate legs. In another minute, the leg would be reduced to the width of a toothpick.

And Isaac would topple to the floor right in front of this ruthless rabbit.

"Think of something," pleaded Isaac. "Somebody think of something fast!"

"How else do we turn it off? How do we turn it off??" Oscar asked no one in particular, but little piles of sawdust were forming at the base of the dresser, and Isaac was already starting to slide.

"The light!" Raj yelled from the headboard, momentarily losing his grip on the ledge and catching himself. "The box said it freezes under light!"

"My flashlight's in the hallway!" screamed Isaac, sliding inches closer to the rabbit.

It took Oscar far too long to remember he was holding the other flashlight.

"Oscar, now!" Raj hollered, and Oscar regained his senses and flipped the beam on the Plushtrap Chaser, but it didn't work.

"Get in front of it!" screamed Isaac, and Oscar scooted to the edge of the vanity and stretched his arm as far as he could so the beam of light shone directly into the bunny's eyes. Suddenly, the toy froze mid-gnaw as it opened wide for the last chomp on the dresser leg.

The room grew quiet as the boys gasped for breath, the beam on the bunny shaking under Oscar's trembling grip.

"Keep it steady," Isaac whispered, as though afraid he could wake the beast by sound.

"I'm trying," hissed Oscar.

The dresser was swaying under Isaac, trying to figure out how to stand on three and a half legs, and it wasn't going to hold Isaac for much longer, with or without the Plushtrap chewing away at it.

"I've gotta get down," said Isaac, more to himself than to his friends, but they understood. He was trying to gather the courage.

"It can't move as long as Oscar keeps the light on it," said Raj, sensing Isaac's distrust of the momentary armistice.

"Easy for you to say," said Isaac, never taking his eyes off the green thing at the base of the wardrobe. "You're not inches from a freaking wood chipper. And what the heck is up with its teeth? They're not supposed to be like that!"

"I think it's safe to say there's a whole lot about this situation that 'isn't supposed to be like that,'" said Raj. "Now, would you get off the stupid dresser?"

"He's right," Oscar encouraged. "So long as there's light, it's not supposed to be able to move."

"It wasn't supposed to be able to move anyway, remember?" said Isaac. "How did it suddenly come to life?"

Neither Raj nor Oscar had a good answer to offer, especially not in that moment.

"Maybe the lightning? Something about when it was plugged into that socket? I don't know. What I do know is that the dresser is about a second from collapsing," said Oscar.

Isaac nodded, accepting his fate. He was going to have to venture down to the floor.

Sliding himself as far away as possible from the open mouth of the Plushtrap, Isaac draped one leg over the side of the dresser, then snatched it back, throwing his balance off.

"Man, come on," said Raj, the suspense killing him.

"Hey, *you* pick which limb *you'd* rather have torn off," growled Isaac, and Oscar tried a different approach.

"Quick and easy, just like a bandage," he suggested, and Isaac seemed to like that approach better.

"Quick and easy," Isaac repeated. Just as Isaac prepared to slide down the dresser, from the far corner of the room—a corner where no one stood—a voice called out:

"Guys, over here!"

Not just any voice, though. Raj's voice.

Oscar didn't mean to move the light to the corner. It was instinct.

"Whoa whoa whoa put it back! PUT IT BACK!"

Oscar juggled the flashlight in his hands and swept the beam back to the Plushtrap's gaze just as its teeth prepared to close on Isaac's sliding leg.

"Cute trick, Raj. Think maybe you could practice your ventriloquist act some other time?" said Oscar, struggling to regain his breath.

But Raj simply stare wide-eyed into the corner.

"It wasn't you, was it?" said Isaac, holding his nearly sacrificed leg.

"Oh, come on. Seriously?" said Oscar. "It can mimic voices?"

"Our voices," said Raj, gulping. "To distract us."

The damaged wood under Isaac groaned, and he slid to the ground and ran faster than Oscar had ever seen him move. Then he skittered across the floor and joined Oscar on the vanity.

"Now what?" asked Raj, and Oscar was ready with an answer.

"We leave the flashlight right here, right on it," he said. "We barricade the door and call for help."

Isaac and Raj thought it over for a second, then silently agreed.

Raj moved first, inching his way off the headboard and backing toward the door, never taking his eyes from the demented bunny, which, under the glow of Oscar's flashlight, had taken on a sickly green hue amid the surrounding shadows of the room.

Then, just as Oscar and Isaac began to lower themselves to the carpet, too, the beam from the flashlight began to falter, flickering on and off in split-second intervals. Panicked, Oscar slapped the side of the light and brought the beam back to life, but only for a second, when it once again failed and reappeared.

"Oscar," said Isaac in a low voice. "Is there any chance at all that wasn't the battery on your flashlight dying?"

The beam blinked out and reappeared again, but it stayed extinguished long enough this time for them to hear the jaw of the Plushtrap shut.

"Um . . ." Oscar started, but he didn't have time to finish. When the beam flickered out this time, it stayed out.

"RUN!" screamed Oscar, and he and Isaac clamored for the door, so close to Raj that they scraped his heels with their toes.

They ran across the hall to the bathroom, and Isaac kicked his dropped flashlight ahead of them. They slammed the door, throwing their backs against it just in time to feel the force of three feet of metal and plush hit the other side. The rabbit wasted no time in running its cracked teeth across the wood, again tackling the area right around the doorknob.

Isaac dropped to the ground and groped for his lost flashlight, juggling it between his hands before finding the switch and casting the beam toward the door. But they all knew it would only work on the bunny once it had chewed through the door.

Once they were face-to-face with it.

"Raj, where's your phone?" said Oscar.

Raj held it up like a talisman, its screen glowing blue in the dark bathroom.

"Save the light," said Oscar. "Just call for help."

"Right," said Raj, catching on. He quickly dialed 9-1-1 and waited for the relief that would come in the form of the operator's voice.

"What's taking so long?" said Isaac, eyeing the handle as it began to wiggle in its loosening support.

"Nothing's happening," said Raj, trying again.

"What do you mean? It's 9-1-1. Someone has to pick up," said Isaac.

"I mean the call's not even going through. Like, there's no service or something, I don't know!" said Raj, growing desperate.

"Okay okay," said Oscar, trying to think it through, but the Plushtrap's teeth were starting to show through the door again. It was leaving tiny green threads on the splinters around the doorknob. "Here's what we're gonna do. I'm going to open the door—"

"Bad idea," Raj said, panic lacing his voice. "Horrible idea."

"Wait," said Oscar, trying to keep his cool. "I'll open the door, and I'll hit it with the light to freeze it. You two get out while I'm shining the light on it and go to the kitchen. You can call for help using the landline."

"So you're saying we should just leave you alone with this thing?!" said Isaac.

"Unless you want to stay here with me," said Oscar.

"No, no, no, we'll go to the kitchen," Raj interjected quickly.

"On my mark," said Oscar, absolutely not ready to call the mark, but it was happening one way or the other; the knob was about to drop.

"Three . . . two . . . ," said Oscar, and he grabbed the doorknob before it lost its place in the door. "GO!"

Oscar flung the door open. The Plushtrap Chaser burst through and went stiff in the light. Its eyes were so muddy under the close beam of the flashlight that it was difficult to remember they used to be green. The featureless orbs were somehow more terrifying than normal live eyeballs. Its mouth hung open hungrily, the teeth even bloodier than they had been the last time Oscar had looked at them closely. Its jointed arms extended straight in front of it, ready to push through the door.

Shallow breaths filled the tiny bathroom as Isaac and Raj jockeyed for space as far away from the Plushtrap as possible, but it was standing in the doorway. They'd have to squeeze past.

Isaac sucked his stomach in, but the wiry hair of the rabbit still grabbed at his shirt. Raj winced and did the same, the top of the rabbit's arm brushing his ear as he scooted past and stood on shaking legs in the hallway with Isaac.

"You're sure about this?" Raj asked Oscar.

"Nope," Oscar said. "Just hurry."

The boys scampered down the hall and yanked the receiver off the phone's cradle in the kitchen. But as Oscar stood eye to bulging eye with the Plushtrap, he could tell by the way his friends were arguing that they weren't getting through to 9-1-1 by the landline either.

When they reappeared in the doorway, Raj was the one to deliver the bad news.

"The phone lines must be down."

As though as confirmation, wind whipped against the house, rattling the space behind the walls where pipes snaked through insulation.

"So to recap," said Oscar, his light carefully trained on the bunny. "We're trapped in my house with a mindless eating machine with exactly one working flashlight—"

"Two if you count my phone," Raj interrupted.

"During a storm that's knocked out the power lines and the phone lines."

"And the water," said Isaac, and the two boys waited for explanation.

"I got thirsty. I tried the tap."

"It can chew through almost anything, so . . ." said Raj.

". . . so what happens when our lights run out of batteries?" said Oscar.

The boys all stared at the Plushtrap as though it might provide an answer. It merely stared into the light Oscar didn't dare take away from its face.

"Hey, Oscar," said Raj, and Oscar didn't like the tone of his voice; it was obvious some new horror had just occurred to him.

"What?"

"How are you going to get out of there?"

"What do you mean? Same way you guys did."

"Uh uh," said Raj, shaking his head slowly. "We got out because you were shining the light on its face."

"Yeah?"

"We're not facing it anymore. We're behind it."

Oscar finally understood. The light didn't just need to be on the rabbit.

"It needs to *see* it," he said, shuddering at the prospect of those horrible dead human eyes seeing anything.

"Hang on," said Isaac. "We can use the mirror."

The boys tried to angle the Plushtrap toward the counter while Oscar's hands made the beam tremble.

"Hold it steady," said Isaac.

"I'm trying. Do you know how hard it is to hold something level for this long? My arm is killing me."

"Would you two shut up!" said Raj, leaning hard against the Plushtrap. "Isaac, help me with this thing."

"Dude, it's not that heavy."

Raj stood away from the rabbit. "You try."

But Isaac couldn't make it budge either.

"It's like its gears are locked in place or something."

They were quiet for another minute.

"Okay, here's what we're going to do," said Oscar. "One of you is going to hold the flashlight over its head, between the ears."

"Not it," said Raj.

"I'll sneak past, and then we'll all make a run for it."

Raj nodded. "Yeah, that could work. As soon as it turns around, we just back away, keep the flashlight on it for as long as we can."

"Exactly. It'll buy us time to at least get down to the end of the hall."

It was the best idea they could muster. And it might have worked if the smaller, cheaper flashlight hadn't begun to flicker in that exact moment. The Great Power Outage of May had drained the batteries prematurely.

"Nonononononono!" said Oscar.

"Why do all your flashlights die??" accused Isaac.

"Shut up and hold it!" said Oscar, and they were all beginning to panic. Isaac cringed as he held his arm between the scratchy fur of the rabbit's ears, angling to beam into its bulging eyes as Oscar flattened himself against the doorframe.

"Lemme in, I'll use my phone light," Raj said breathlessly.

"Too late," said Isaac. "No room to switch places."

Then, just as Oscar was pinned beside the Plushtrap, they heard a voice from the front door.

"Little man, I need your help!"

"Ms. Avila!" Isaac called over his shoulder. "Stay there, don't move!"

But it was Isaac who moved, just a little as he turned, but enough to move the beam of his light.

"Isaac, the light!" Oscar yelled.

"Sorry!" Isaac refocused the light on the rabbit, but his arm shook, and the beam began to falter, creating a deeply unsettling strobe effect. Now, the rabbit's head slowly turned in increments, during the dark intervals between the flashlight's beam.

When Oscar was nose-to-nose with the rabbit, the flash-light failed completely.

"RUUUUUUUN!" screamed Oscar, and the others followed suit, shrieking in unison as the Plushtrap lived up to its name, chasing them in freakishly smooth mechanical strides down the narrow hallway of Oscar's house.

Raj tried to aim his phone screen behind him, but the beam of light wasn't bright enough.

"The flashlight!" yelled Isaac, and Raj tried, but in his panic, the thin phone slipped right through his sweating hands.

If there was any hope that the phone had survived its fall, the immediate crunch that came afterward extinguished that hope. The rabbit had stomped it.

"The garage!" Oscar managed to gasp as they fled the biggest regret of his life.

Throwing the door closed against the lunging rabbit, the boys listened in horror as it once again began to attack its obstacle with ruthless efficiency.

"This is the world's worst toy!" Raj gasped.

"How did it know your mom's voice?" Isaac wheezed.

"Who knows?" Oscar said, throwing his hands in the air. "Maybe it overheard her on the phone?" He laughed hyster-ically. "The possibilities are endless!"

Isaac clapped a hand over Oscar's shoulder. "Snap out of it, man. You're losing it."

Unlike the other rooms of the house that had at least the

benefit of shadows to see the space around them, the garage was pitch black, and as the boys groped for something they could use against the intruder, they managed only to knock tools off of shelves and trip over stored Christmas decorations.

"I suppose it's too much to ask if you have another flashlight in here somewhere?" Isaac asked, his voice raspy with fear.

"Even if there was, I wouldn't know where to find it," said Oscar.

Raj slapped at the garage door button frantically, but with the power out, it was no use.

"Don't these things have an emergency release?" he asked, logic finally prevailing.

Fur and teeth were beginning to emerge through the chewed hole in the door to the garage.

"There's a lever!" said Oscar, groping toward where he thought the middle of the garage might be. "It should be somewhere right . . ."

He began jumping, stretching his hands high overhead as he swiped at the air, searching for the knob tied to the rope that released the emergency lock on the garage.

Raj joined him in the hunt, taking a different place in the garage.

"Guys," Isaac said, and his voice was unsettlingly calm.

"Hang on, I think my finger just hit it!" said Oscar.

"Guys," said Isaac again.

"Where?" said Raj.

"Over here."

"Where's here?"

"*Here!*"

"Guys!" said Isaac, and this time, they both paused to listen. The sound of scraping began to grow louder as the Plushtrap made quick work of the thicker wood of the garage door.

"What?" they answered in unison.

"Where are we gonna go after this?"

Oscar understood at some primal level why Isaac sounded so defeated. With no light anywhere to be found, all they could do was . . . run.

"So what, we just hang out and get ground up into hamburger?" said Raj, resuming jumping.

Oscar's terror reached a new level when Isaac didn't have an answer.

And to think—less than an hour ago, their most vexing question had been about which end of the train tracks to start their trick-or-treating on.

"The train!" yelled Oscar, and just as he did, he heard Raj's hand connect with the wooden knob and string attached to the garage's emergency release. The knob slapped the metal of the garage door. Raj jumped again, and again he sent the knob swinging.

"There it is!"

"You guys!" Isaac yelled, urgency finding him once

more, and they watched wide-eyed as the doorknob in the door began to wobble.

"He's almost—" said Isaac.

"I'm almost—" said Raj.

Isaac's voice laughed from the other side of the door.

"This is it. I'm putting you out of your misery in three, two, and you're de—"

Raj's fingertips caught the wooden knob, and this time, he yanked hard on the string, releasing the automatic arm holding the garage door in place.

"Get on that side!" said Oscar, and Isaac grabbed the ridge of the garage door on one end while Raj took the middle and Oscar took the left.

They flung the garage door up with enough force to make it hit the top of its track and come crashing back down. Just as it did, the handle from the door leading to the garage dropped to the concrete floor, and the door swung wide to reveal the Plushtrap Chaser, set on its mindless destruction.

The boys threw the garage door open with the same amount of force, only this time, they ducked underneath before it came crashing down again, putting them on the driveway and the rabbit in the garage.

It slammed into the door, dragging its teeth across the metal as they winced under the sound.

"This isn't going to hold it for long," said Raj, and while the Oscar from yesterday might have doubted that even a functioning Plushtrap could cut through metal, the Oscar of tonight had every reason to believe it. It wouldn't stop until it had a reason to.

"The train," he said again, then took off running, taking it on faith that the other two would follow him.

They'd barely reached the end of Oscar's block before they heard the squeal of twisted metal and knew their borrowed time had expired.

They hurdled over bikes left abandoned in people's yards and electrical transformer boxes, swatting away dead leaves and trash that swirled in the air and assaulted them, all to the soundtrack of a steadily moving mechanical rabbit, its jaw opening and slamming shut to the increasing speed of its chasing legs. Oscar dared to look behind him only once, finding the Plushtrap closer than he'd feared it might be. Close enough to see the glowing whites of its vacant eyes.

As the rabbit gained speed, Oscar and his friends lost theirs. The train tracks were still a quarter of a mile away.

"Do I even wanna know how close it is?" Raj asked, his breathing quickly transitioning to wheezing.

"Just keep going," said Oscar. "Whatever you do, don't slow down."

Oscar's legs burned as he pumped his arms, but even Isaac was starting to peter out. They just needed to make it a little farther.

"How . . ." Isaac panted, swallowing before trying again. "How do you even know there'll be a train?"

Isaac had guessed the plan Oscar didn't have time to explain.

"I don't," said Oscar, and Isaac didn't say a word after that. He understood.

If there wasn't a train, then there wasn't any hope.

Dipping into the clearest path they could find in the wooded land leading to the train tracks, Oscar, Isaac, and Raj raised their hands over their heads, shielding their faces from low-hanging branches as they listened to the Plushtrap crash a path through the trees, making quick work of any branches that dared to get in its way.

When the path began to incline, Oscar knew they were getting close. His lungs were on fire, and Raj was beginning to cough and sputter in pain.

When they crested the hill, Oscar saw the most glorious of all sights.

Light.

"I told you!" Isaac panted. "They never lose power!"

But as they tumbled down the slope leading toward the tracks, they once again lost sight of the east side of town, and the dreadful realization struck Oscar that without a train to intervene, they'd never make it to the east side in all of its lighted glory.

The sound was faint at first, nearly impossible to hear over the howl of the storm and the buzz saw of the Plushtrap gaining on them. But when Raj and Isaac looked in the same direction, Oscar thought he heard it; he knew it wasn't just a phantom noise.

"The train horn. It's coming. It's coming!" yelled Isaac, and they yelled a collective *whoop*, filled with relief at hearing their savior approach.

But they couldn't see it yet. And when they turned around, what they did see froze Oscar's blood in his veins. The shadow of a rabbit loomed tall across their feet before the bunny ascended the top of the hill.

"It's not going to come in time," whispered Isaac.

"It'll come in time," said Oscar.

The Plushtrap tipped forward at the hill's peak and launched, sprinting down the hill with expert, deadly precision.

"We're gonna die. This is it, we're gonna die," said Raj.

"It'll come in time," said Oscar, never taking his eyes off the rabbit.

It was halfway down the hill before Oscar heard the beautiful sound of the train's horn cutting through the whir of the storm.

The rabbit's eyes bulged, its ears stuck straight in the air at an unnatural angle. And as it pounded down the second half of the hill, Oscar could even see shards of mangled metal from the garage door sticking out of its jagged teeth like chicken bones.

Oscar dared to take his eyes from the Plushtrap just long

enough to catch sight of a small circle of light at the visible end of the track.

"Go," Oscar said to them.

"No way, man," said Raj. "All of us together."

"Just trust me," said Oscar.

"Are you nuts??" said Isaac.

"Get across the tracks," Oscar said, a strange calm washing over his body as he measured the distance in each periphery of his vision—the oncoming Plushtrap and the oncoming train. His brain was doing calculus he didn't even know it was capable of.

The horn blared through the air. The train was mere seconds away. So was the Plushtrap.

"Guys, it's going to work. This time, it's all going to work out. Just go!"

Raj and Isaac took one more look at the oncoming train before diving over the tracks and tumbling to the other side.

Oscar could hear them screaming for him to cross, too. He could hear them, but he wasn't listening. All he could focus on in that moment—in that split second between possible life and certain death—was the crackling but stubbornly alive voice of Mr. Devereaux.

Sometimes you have to know when to go for it, even when it doesn't look possible.

And in that impossibly small and infinitely huge space of time, Oscar finally understood what the old man meant:

Sometimes luck isn't found. Sometimes luck is made. And when it is, you had to know when to grab hold of it.

To the chorus of his friends' screams and the blaring of the train's horn and the grinding of the rabbit's teeth, he took three giant steps to the right toward the train, stepped onto the tracks, and waited for just the right second when the Plushtrap Chaser raced onto the tracks and turned to face Oscar and the bright beam of the train's light.

Oscar had a split second to register the sinister eyes. From its ravenous, bloody mouth came the voice of Oscar's mom:

"Little man, I need you!"

Then Oscar jumped.

The air surrounding him smelled of steel and fire, and at first, he didn't know what to make of the light. Was he in a hospital? Was he trapped under the train?

"Did I die?" he heard his voice in his ears, and it seemed detached from his body.

"Honestly, I don't know how, but no," said Raj, gulping at the air on the east side of the tracks, his body trembling hard enough for Oscar to feel the ground shaking under him. Or maybe that was the train. He could still hear the blare of the horn in the distance.

Oscar looked to Isaac, whose hands were on his knees as he closed his eyes and shook his head slowly.

"You're an idiot," he said.

"I know," said Oscar.

But once the ground stopped vibrating and their legs stopped wobbling, they crept over to the part of the track where Oscar had played his most dangerous game of chicken.

There, twisted and flattened into the concrete ties and hardened soil underneath, lay the remains of one Plushtrap Chaser, a light-activated chomping green rabbit and no longer Oscar's favorite character from the Freddy Fazbear world. Dark green fur floated in clouds around the smashed rabbit, while other clumps stuck with grease to the rail ties. Tiny jagged pieces of teeth shone under the newly uncovered moon, the clouds finally parting after it was already too late to help. Bits of bloody human gum were attached to the teeth. Oscar swallowed down bile and shifted his gaze.

Oscar stared down at the single grotesque eye that remained semi-intact, half buried but still bulging from the packed earth under the track. The other eye was smashed tissue, dead, but looking more human than ever. He shivered and turned to walk away. He was unable to stand looking at such an unblinking killer.

The next night, Oscar helped deliver candy to the residents at the Royal Oaks Nursing Home while his mom lit fires under the orderlies and rolled her eyes at the newest, dumbest ones. It was a sort of reverse trick-or-treating, with the candy coming to the people since they couldn't come for the candy. When Oscar arrived at Mr. Devereaux's room, Marilyn was curled at the foot of his bed.

"Someone's feeling bold," Oscar said to her, but Mr. Devereaux was the one who answered.

"I've decided that if she's going to steal my soul, she's earned the right," he said, and while it made zero sense to Oscar, it seemed to make enough sense to Mr. Devereaux that he no longer eyed the loyal cat with suspicion.

"So, how'd the harvest go?" he asked, and again, Oscar found himself in the company of one of Mr. Devereaux's lucid moments. More than lucid, even. It's like he'd been standing right there on the train tracks with Oscar when he needed it most.

"Bad crop this year," he said, and Mr. Devereaux nodded slowly, as though he'd been there before. Oscar tried and failed to imagine Mr. Devereaux with his own three-foot-tall chomping rabbit.

"But I'm glad I did the digging," said Oscar, and with that, Mr. Devereaux was satisfied enough to fall back asleep, Marilyn greedily kneading the space between his splayed feet.

In the break room, Oscar found his mother, to whom he hadn't spoken since the morning, and only to explain that the toy had done "just a little bit of damage" to the doors, and he'd spend the next weekend patching them and probably the rest of his natural life saving for a new garage door. His mom hardly seemed to notice, though. He supposed their fight over the phone earlier in the night had left more of a gaping hole in her than anything the Plushtrap could have done.

Because he'd felt so awful about that, he did something that he knew wouldn't make up for it, but he knew he had to try. So he took what remained of his money and stopped into HAL'S HALLOWEEN HALLWAY and picked up a small plastic jack-o'-lantern and two bags of the chocolate-covered almonds she loved so much. He filled the pumpkin with the chocolates and stashed it in a cabinet in the break room until he knew she'd be taking her first coffee of the night.

When he handed it to her, she smiled, but he thought she hadn't looked that sad since his dad died.

Still, she pulled him in for the tightest, rib-cracking hug in recent memory, and even though he could barely breathe under her fierce grip, he was so happy to know that he hadn't completely destroyed her.

"I never meant to depend on you so much," she whispered while she held him, and Oscar was surprised. He'd thought his dad was the reason for her sadness. He'd never considered *she* might be the reason.

"It's okay," and he surprised himself by meaning it. It really was okay. Not all the time, but he thought maybe that made the good times better. Like when his mom liked the present he made for her. Or when his friends put their actual lives on the line just so he wouldn't face a monster alone.

"It's okay," he said, and he let her hug him for a good long while.

ABOUT THE AUTHORS

Scott Cawthon is the author of the bestselling video game series *Five Nights at Freddy's*, and while he is a game designer by trade, he is first and foremost a storyteller at heart. He is a graduate of The Art Institute of Houston and lives in Texas with his wife and four sons.

Andrea Rains Waggener is an author, novelist, ghost-writer, essayist, short story writer, screenwriter, copywriter, editor, poet, and a proud member of Kevin Anderson & Associates' team of writers. In a past she prefers not to remember much, she was a claims adjuster, JCPenney's catalogue order-taker (before computers!), appellate court clerk, legal writing instructor, and lawyer. Writing in genres that vary from her chick-lit novel, *Alternate Beauty*, to her dog how-to book, *Dog Parenting*, to her self-help book, *Healthy, Wealthy, and Wise*, to ghostwritten memoirs to ghostwritten YA, horror, mystery, and mainstream fiction projects, Andrea still manages to find time to watch the rain and obsess over her dog and her knitting, art, and music projects. She lives with her husband and said dog on the Washington Coast, and if she isn't at home creating something, she can be found walking on the beach.

Carly Anne West is the author of YA novels *The Murmurings* and *The Bargaining* and middle grade novels based on the *Hello Neighbor* video games. She lives in Seoul, South Korea, with her husband and their two sons.

Grim wasn't always lucid.

Well now, it wasn't good to fib. The truth was that Grim was *rarely* lucid. Being lucid made his teeth hurt. His teeth hurt when his eyes and his ears hurt. When he was lucid, the world had this way of assaulting his eyes and his ears. Everything was too intense, too much. Grim preferred to hang out in his own crazy world where the voices in his head ruled, even when he knew they were crazy.

Grim's teeth hurt tonight.

In the shadows, pressed against the corrugated metal sides of a storage shed near the train tracks, Grim pulled his dirty pink acrylic blanket tighter around his body. Though the blanket was damp and provided no warmth, it comforted him. Also, because it wasn't just dirty—it was so filthy you had to pry at the blanket fibers with a fingernail to find a hint of pink—it gave him camouflage. Camouflage was good. Ever since he'd walked away from his life, he'd done everything he could to be invisible: he hunched his five feet eight inches into several inches less than that; he ate just enough to keep skin hanging on his bones; he covered his long stringy brown hair with a floppy gray hat; he hid his long face under a matted beard. And he gave up his name for the nickname he'd been given. He made it his goal to be unseen.

He especially did not want to be seen right now. No way. No how.

He didn't want to be seen because he didn't like the pounding and clanking. And he didn't like what he was seeing. He was seeing ominous things, things that hurt his teeth.

For the last five minutes, Grim's gaze had been riveted on the railroad tracks. Or again—truth was important— not on the tracks themselves but rather what was *on* the tracks. What was on the tracks was disturbing him greatly.

On the tracks, illuminated by the peripheral glow of a security light, a cloaked figure was prying bizarre items from the rails. The figure was slightly hunched and moving in an awkward pitch-and-roll gait that reminded Grim of the way people walked after coming off a boat. Grim was only twenty feet or so from the hooded person, but he could clearly see both the figure and what it was collecting.

The person appeared to be unaware of Grim, and Grim intended to keep it that way. Grim's teeth wanted to chatter, and his body wanted to shake, but he willed himself still as he watched the mysterious figure pound at the end of what looked like a foot-long pry bar with a bright yellow end. The yellow end kept wriggling free pieces of something Grim couldn't identify. So far he'd seen it collect a hinged jaw, a jagged row of what looked like bloody human teeth, mutilated human eyes, several bolts, a computer port, and chunks of metal with tufts of dark green fur.

Now he continued to watch while the figure pried up one and then two green oblong objects. What were those?

As if answering Grim's inner question, the figure held up the pieces. Even in the muted light, Grim could immediately discern what they were. In his previous life, he'd been a professor, and even at the rate he'd been pickling his brain cells, he still had many at his disposal.

Green rabbit ears.

Oh, his teeth.

The figure went back to prying, and it worked free of the tracks a large metal rabbit foot.

Grim had to admit to himself a modicum of curiosity about what the figure was doing. But his sense of self-preservation was stronger. So he sat, with aching teeth, as still as the bits of detritus the figure was collecting, until the figure put all the pried-up parts in a bag and disappeared into the darkness.

Detective Larson knocked on the door of a one-and-a-half-story brown Craftsman house squatting next to a two-story Craftsman four times its size. He looked down at the well-maintained porch he stood on. It looked like it had fresh paint. He'd noticed the entire house was in similar condition. But the paint and tidiness weren't having what was probably their intended effect. The house he stood in front of looked diminished, not just in relation to its bigger, spiffier neighbor, but in general. If houses had faces, this house would look hangdog.

A mission-style door opened in front of Larson. A pretty young woman with almost cartoon-large eyes and shoulder-length brown hair looked at the detective with absolutely no interest. "Yes?"

"Ma'am, my name is Detective Larson." He showed the woman his shield. She gave it the same non-attention she was giving him. "As part of an ongoing routine investigation, I need to take a look at the premises. Do you have any objections?"

The woman squinted at him. He thought he saw the glint of something lying dormant in her gaze, like she had some spark that had been nearly, but not fully, extinguished. He wondered if that spark was about to light an objection to his entry. He didn't know what he'd do if it did because he didn't have a warrant.

The woman shrugged. "Come on in."

Crossing the threshold into a meticulously clean and neat living room, he looked around and saw that a small kitchen and dining room were in similar condition—this in spite of the fact that the house contained at least four cats, which lounged in various displays of regal ownership on the backs of furniture or in puddles of sunlight on braided throw rugs.

"I'm Margie," the woman said. She offered her hand.

Larson took it. It was cool and limp.

She looked up at him, one eyebrow raised, as if she was waiting for him to answer some unasked question. He smiled at her but said nothing. He wondered what she saw when she looked at him. Did she see the thirty-something, decent-looking guy he used to see in himself or did she see the deep lines forming around his mouth and eyes, which was all he could see now when he caught a glimpse of his face in the mirror?

She looked away, her gaze landing on two of the cats. She frowned and shook her head. "Sorry about all the cats. I'm not sure how this happened. I was given one to keep me company after . . . um, well, just to keep me company. Turned out it was a she, and she was pregnant. I couldn't bear to give the four kittens away. I felt like their mom, and it seemed like abandonment. So here I am. A cat lady." She gave a dry laugh and then coughed.

Larson had a feeling she used to laugh a lot and had gotten out of practice lately. He wondered what had happened to her. He was tempted to ask, but that wasn't why he was here.

Larson started wandering through the house. Margie followed him.

"How long have you lived here?" he asked. He'd found that chatting with homeowners tended to distract them when he was checking out their place. It gave him more time to poke around before they started getting uncomfortable or even defensive.

"Just over three years." Her voice hitched between "three" and "years."

He glanced at her.

She sounded like she was going to cry, but her eyes were dry, and her face was placid. "I was hired to take care of a sick boy while his dad served overseas. He passed away and left me the house."

The dad or the boy, Larson wondered. He didn't ask.

Larson had stepped into a short hallway with three doors. A fifth cat appeared from inside the last door. It was a small gray tabby. It sat down in the middle of the hall and started cleaning itself.

Larson looked into a small, shiny bathroom and then into a decent-size bedroom, the one the woman was obviously using. A fuzzy yellow robe was folded neatly at the foot of a queen bed, and cosmetics were lined up just as neatly on a cherry dresser. Other than those touches, he thought the room had a distinctly masculine feel.

Larson decided not to comment on the woman's relationship with her dead employer, whatever that relationship might have been. He didn't need to risk setting her on edge. He continued on down the hall.

The old house creaked and shifted, emitting something that sounded like a groan. He was pretty sure Margie flinched at the noise.

A dark gray cat meandered down the hall, sniffed the gray tabby, and then rubbed against Larson's black slacks. He bent over and scratched it behind the ears. He knew he'd be sorry later. He was allergic to cats, but he still liked them.

Stepping into what was obviously the second bedroom, Larson stared at the single bed in the middle of the room. Other than the bed, the room held only a small cabinet.

He wasn't sure what to make of this room, but he was compelled to stay in it. Specifically, the cabinet grabbed his attention.

Next to him, Margie was quiet. She was close enough for him to smell what he assumed was her soap or shampoo. It had a fresh but clean scent, nothing heavy or alluring like perfume or cologne. In spite of the makeup she wore, he got the impression Margie didn't care much about doing things to impress others. He wondered if that was why he found her attractive. He liked her simple transparency. No, she wasn't spilling her guts to him in the annoying way nervous witnesses often did, but she wasn't trying to be something she wasn't either. He could tell.

He cleared his throat as he meandered around the bed toward the cabinet that had captured his interest. "We've been pursuing a person of interest in the ongoing case I mentioned. The case has been at a near standstill. It's gone without any leads, until recently. Now we have this." He reached into the inner pocket of his gray sports jacket and pulled out a photo, which he held up for Margie to see.

Margie said nothing, but her face had a lot to say. First, she flushed. Then, as quickly as her cheeks went pink they lost all color, and she blanched. Her eyes widened. Her mouth opened slightly. He heard her breathing quicken.

About to call her out on her reaction, Detective Larson did a stutter step of surprise when the gray tabby suddenly jumped onto the single bed.

"Sorry," Margie said again. She picked up the cat. It immediately started purring.

Larson couldn't help himself. He reached out and rubbed the side of its face. Suddenly aware he was very close to Margie, he stepped back.

The cabinet was right in front of him. He hadn't realized he'd reached it. Now, he had to see what was inside of it.

At the same time he was drawn to it, he felt an inexplicable reluctance to open the cabinet door. He sneezed.

"Excuse me," he said.

"It's the cats," Margie said.

"It's okay." He was lying. He'd be miserable the rest of the day.

He realized he was putting off opening the cabinet. Which was absurd. So he grabbed the cabinet knob and pulled on it.

The cabinet was empty, but the inside walls of the cabinet weren't. They were covered in harsh black scribblings jammed close together. What looked like nonsensical letters made by a thick marker covered nearly every inch of the cabinet's interior. Larson could see no meaning in the scrawls, but nonetheless they gave him the same feeling he'd had when he'd looked at the recent grotesque death reports.

Larson turned and looked at Margie. "What happened in this house?"

A DEADLY SECRET IS LURKING AT THE HEART OF FREDDY FAZBEAR'S PIZZA...

Unravel the twisted mysteries behind the bestselling horror video games and the *New York Times* bestselling series.